"Audrey?" Bradley asks.

I blink and realize he must have been talking to me.

"I'm sorry. I was thinking about something else." I do it all the time. My family is used to it and it doesn't bother them, but he's looking at me like something's wrong with me.

"I was just asking how much milk you like in your coffee."

"Oh," I say. "Enough so it doesn't taste like coffee. Or motor oil." Geez. I'm not fit to be around other people. Brianna and Lilah were right. I should have brought them.

Bradley gives me a little grin, then as he makes the coffee, I twist at my wedding ring.

He'd asked about my husband. People are going to ask. I'm going to have to tell them. There's no way around it.

Bradley hands me a cup of hot coffee. I take it from him and set it on counter.

"You asked what brought me to Whiskey Springs."

"Just making conversation. You don't have to answer."

"This house belonged to my husband's grandfather."

"Theodore Albright."

"Yes. And now it apparently belongs to me."

Bradley sets his mug down, too. Leans a hip against the kitchen island and studies me.

"Last I heard it belonged to a fellow named Thomas Albright. He sold it to you?"

"No. I inherited it."

He tilts his head to the side and looks at me. "I'm a little confused now."

"Thomas Albright was my husband."

"Was." I can see him putting things together. *Was. Inherited.*

"I know it's confusing because I didn't take his name."

"Not unusual."

Apparently somehow word about Thomas's accident had not traveled to Whiskey Springs.

"Thomas Albright was killed in an airplane crash two weeks ago." I straighten my shoulders and force myself to follow through with the words. "I'm his widow."

JUST BREATHE

THE GRAVITY OF US SERIES

KATHRYN KALEIGH

The Gravity of Us Series

(Reading Order)

Just Breathe

Just Surface

Just Melt

All of the books in the Gravity of Us Series are

standalone and can be read out of order.

However, the books are linked

and are best when read in order.

Also by Kathryn Kaleigh

Contemporary

(ALPINE FALLS)

Secrets and Second Chances

Honeymoon with a Stranger

Not Our Wedding

Stranded in Alpine Falls

Belonging in Alpine Falls

The Spirit of Christmas in Alpine Falls

Christmas Wishes in Alpine Falls

Finding True North in Alpine Falls

A Ghost of Christmas Magic in Alpine Falls

(SILVER PINES)

The Way Back to You

Back to Where We Began

When We Were Us

(ONCE UPON FOREVER)

My Forever Guy

Our Forever Love

Forever Vows

Finding Forever

Accidentally Forever

(TRUE NORTH)

Borrowed Until Monday

Still Mine

The Moon and the Stars at Christmas

Perfectly Mismatched

On the Way to Forever

A Merry Little Christmas

On the Way Home to Christmas

It was Always You

(UNBREAK MY HEART)

Begin Again

Love Again

Falling Again

(FOR THE LOVE OF THE FLIGHT)

Just Stay

Just Chance

Just Believe

Just Us

Just Once

Just Happened

Just Maybe

Just Pretend

Just Because

(MAGNETIC NORTH)

Second Chance Kisses

Second Chance Secrets

First Time Charm

Three Broken Rules

Second Chance Destiny

Unexpected Vows

(FALLING FOR CHRISTMAS)

The Heart of Christmas

The Magic of Christmas

In a One Horse Open Sleigh

A Secret Royal Christmas

An Old Fashioned Christmas

(CITY SKYLINE BILLIONAIRES)

Billionaire's Unexpected Landing

Billionaire's Accidental Girlfriend

Billionaire's Fallen Angel

Billionaire's Secret Crush

Billionaire's Barefoot Bride

(TRULY, MADLY, DEEPLY)

The Lady in the Red Dress

On the Edge of Chance

Sealed with a Kiss

Kiss Me at Midnight

The Heart Knows

(STOLEN ECHOES)

When Cupid's Arrow Strikes

Chasing Fireflies

A Chance Encounter

(EDGE OF THE HORIZON)

The Forever Equation

Pretend Boyfriend

All our Tomorrows

Kissing for Keeps

Out of the Blue

The Princess and the Playboy

(RED LIPSTICK KISSES)

Red Lipstick Kisses and Small Town Wishes

Stolen Dances and Big City Chances

Chance Connections and Upside Down Plans

A Christmas Kiss on the Twenty-Fifth

Believe in the Magic of Christmas

Vows of Inheritance Series

(Reading Order)

Vow to Protect

Vow to Redeem

All of the books in each Series are standalone and can be read out of order. However, some books have characters from the previous stories in them.

ALSO BY KATHRYN KALEIGH

ROMANTASY

(IN THE SPIRIT OF LOVE)

Spirits of the Heart

Out of Dreams and Ashes

Etched Upon the Heart

WESTERN ROMANCE

(LONE STAR HEARTS)

Wanted by a Texas Ranger

Saved by a Texas Ranger

(WHISKEY SPRINGS)

Finding Natalie

Promising Samantha

Falling for Allyson

Saving Savannah

Claiming Charlie

Rescuing Keira

Protecting Gabriella

Courting Isabella

TIME TRAVEL

(INTO THE MIST)

Written in the Wind

Scripted in the Stars

Destined in the Twilight

Promised in the Mist

Trapped in the Melody

(DRAGON'S BLOOD)

Dragon's Blood

Lavender Blue

Champagne Silver

Twilight Frost

Mountbatten Pink

(WHEN HEARTSTRINGS BECKON)

Rescued in Time

Meet me in 1879

(WHEN HEARTSTRINGS ECHO)

Messages Across Time

Falling Through to Forever

Once Upon a Winter's Spell

(BECKONED)

Before the Storm

Twist of Fate

When the Stars Align

Once Upon a Christmas

Once in a Blue Moon

A Wish Upon a Star

(BEGUILED)

When Lightning Strikes

Storm of Time

Midnight Storm

When the Moon Falls

Stormborn Angel

(SPELLED)

Time Tempest

The Heart Remembers

A Moment in Time

Moonlight Shadows

HISTORICAL

(TAPESTRY OF BLUE AND GRAY)

Shadows Beneath Magnolia Blooms

Secrets Among Southern Roses

(IT HAPPENED BY ACCIDENT)

Accidentally Alluring

Accidentally Married

(SOUTHERN BELLE CIVIL WAR)

Beyond Enemy Lines

Love Always

Hearts Under Siege

Hearts Under Fire

Away Down South in Dixie

The Reluctant Bride

Stay with Me

Jasmine Kisses

Magnolia Kisses

Gardenia Kisses

(THE QUINNS)

Wait for Me

Take Me Home

Keep Me Safe

FATED MATES

Riley's Mate

Aiden's Mate

Brayden's Mate

STANDALONE SUSPENSE

Lost and Found

All I Want for Christmas

Serenity

Courting Alley Cat

JUST BREATHE

CHAPTER
ONE

Audrey
Houston, Texas

I became a widow on a stormy Tuesday evening.

I'd just locked up the art gallery on McKinney Street and pulled out of the parking garage when the sky opened up. Blinding rain hammers the roof of my Toyota Camry, loud and relentless, like the storm had been holding its breath until I left work.

My windshield wipers fight hard, but the downpour blurs everything—the road, the streetlights, the familiar city skyline. Sheets of water pour down the window.

Even through the strong new car scent, I smell the

rain. Clean and fresh. Washing away the dust of southern humidity.

Normally, I like the rain. It makes the world feel quieter, softer somehow. But not tonight.

I slow at the intersection, squinting through the blur of headlights and storm. Typical spring in Texas—clear skies one moment, flooded roads the next.

I dread the drive home. Even with a straight shot on Interstate 10, it's still a long drive out to Katy. It's a mystery to me and probably always will be just why Thomas wanted to buy a house out in the suburbs when I worked downtown and he spent most of his time at the airport north of town.

So every day, often even on weekends, I get in my car and head east toward downtown while he gets in his car and heads north toward the airport.

As an airplane pilot, he spends the night away from home at least once a week. In his defense, I guess he thought I would be safer out in the suburbs. But the drive...

I hadn't complained. Not when the three-story house, all stone and glass, with its manicured lawn was so pretty. And new. The new house with its brand new appliances. No one else has ever lived in it before us. Considering it was my first house after living in apartments, I'm pretty happy once I get inside.

The gallery had hosted an event tonight for two very

different artists. One of them was known for realistic photographs and the other for abstract watercolors.

Two artists, more different in every way possible, couldn't have been paired together even if we'd tried. Concurrent hosting is new. Something suggested by the new CEO to increase profits.

My job was easy. My job was to make sure everyone else did their job. The hostess. The caterer. Other than that, I spent most of my time talking to guests.

When the first phone call from a number I don't recognize shows up on my dashboard screen, I let it go to voicemail. After an evening of talking to people, I just want time to decompress. That's how I typically use the drive home. I'd replay the evening. Catalog everything away in my head and make room for a glass of wine and a book.

Thomas is on an overnight trip tonight to Austin, so it's just me. I'm looking forward to getting out of my heels and cocktail dress, grabbing a glass of wine, and curling up on the sofa in front of the fireplace with a romance novel.

Thomas and I usually watch a movie or binge watch some series or another, but when I'm alone, I'm content to just spend the evening quietly reading. My go to evening activity before I met Thomas.

The second time my phone rings, I hit the button and send the caller straight to voicemail. I don't need a distraction from driving right now. Not in this thunderstorm.

As though to support my decision, a flash of lightning splits the sky just as I merge onto the interstate followed by an ear-splitting crash of thunder that makes the air tremble.

The third time my phone rings, I'm nearing the outer loop, still gripping the steering wheel, cringing as every car rushes past, sending an extra spray of water onto the windshield. A quick glance tells me it's the same number calling. A local number.

My family lives in Atlanta, so it's either a wrong number or work. This time of night, just after ten, I'm going with wrong number.

But it could be someone with a problem related to the art gallery and as the manager, I'm responsible. I press the answer button on my steering wheel.

"Hello."

"Ms. Albright?"

"This is Audrey." I didn't take Thomas's last name and it rather annoys me that people always assume that I did.

Not that there's anything wrong with a woman taking her husband's name. I just hadn't. And it seems like people shouldn't make assumptions.

"This is John with the FAA."

"The FAA." My stomach knots. "I think you meant to call Thomas's number."

He's quiet for a moment. "Are you driving?"

"Yes." Thunder crashes again and I grip the steering wheel with both hands. Despite the rain and diminished visibility, cars and big eighteen wheelers fly past me on either side.

I just want to be home.

"I hear the storm," he says. "Can I call you back?"

"Sure. But Thomas isn't available."

"It's okay," he says. "I'll call you back."

"Sure thing," I say and disconnect the line.

How had John from the FAA gotten my phone number and why is he calling Thomas late at night?

It probably has something to do with Thomas's return flight home tomorrow. Probably delayed. Thomas, like all pilots, has a lot of delayed flights. It comes with the territory.

Thomas and I haven't known each other all that long all in all. We'd worked together a short time on the annual staff in college, but he'd been a senior and I'd been a sophomore. Four years after he'd graduated and moved on, he'd walked into my art gallery. That was about a year ago.

Although he'd remembered me, I hadn't recognized him right away.

Six months later we were married.

Thomas always seemed to be in a hurry to do things. He'd been in a hurry to get married. In a hurry to buy a house. He just didn't have much sense of delayed gratification. I'd teased him about it, finding it a bit endearing.

And he was charming enough that he was able to convince me to go along with most things. With me being one of the least impulsive people I knew, he amused me. I rather liked that he pulled me out of my comfort zone on occasion.

I exit off the freeway and head toward my gated neighborhood.

Katy, oddly enough, typically has more traffic than downtown, but this time of night, the roads are pretty much empty.

I drive through the gate, make the five turns required to get to my house, then pull into the garage. Turn off the motor and open my door to the welcome quiet.

The storm still rages outside, but inside the garage, it's blissfully quiet.

It's usually not so bad going from one garage to the next. Even when it's brutally hot outside. Work to home. The rain, however, makes the drive tricky and tonight was one of the worst storms I've driven through.

But I made it.

I let myself inside and head straight upstairs to the bedroom to change clothes.

Just as I step out of my heels, my phone rings again. I pull it out of my purse and glare at the number.

It's the same number. John from the FAA.

"Hello John," I say. "Do you have my husband's phone number?"

"Yes," he says. "But it's you I need to talk to."

I sit down hard on the little bench in my closet as realization slams into me. Glancing over at Thomas's clothes, neatly hung and organized, I smell his cologne from where he'd gotten dressed earlier in the day.

Thomas always calls when he lands. I'd gotten so busy with the gallery event and then driving in the storm, I only now realized that I hadn't heard from him.

I glance at the time. He should have landed about three hours ago. Three hours.

I'd been so distracted, it hadn't even occurred to me until this minute that he hadn't checked in.

"Why? Has something happened?" I ask, remembering that I'm on the phone with John with the FAA. "He should be in Austin." I have an overwhelming urge to hang up and dial Thomas's phone number. "The storm..."

"Yes. The storm that's over Houston now came down from the west."

"So Thomas got delayed." That would explain things. He got delayed and he didn't call because he knew I had an important event tonight. But that didn't explain why John from the FAA was on the phone with me.

"He didn't get delayed."

I thought for a minute. Thomas had taken me flying plenty of times. He'd taught me some basics. Flight plans. Weather reports. He was careful.

"A detour then. They had to detour him to another airport." Despite my optimist words, there's a knot forming in the pit of my stomach.

"He radioed in with engine trouble."

"Engine trouble? Emergency landing then." Panic is in my voice now replacing the annoyance. My phone is on speaker, but I'm surprised the phone itself doesn't crack with my herculean grip.

"Audrey. We lost contact with your husband's plane about five pm."

Audrey

Two mornings later, I wander downstairs, wearing sweatpants and a t-shirt, my hair pulled back in a messy ponytail, where my two sisters are in the kitchen.

"Who are these people?" I ask, mostly to myself. I don't expect an answer.

There are people in my house. I don't like people in my house.

I didn't invite them.

Neighbors from the looks of them.

People I've never even met.

Sitting on my sofa. Talking in hushed tones. Light chuckles. Furtive glances in my direction.

We stand behind the island looking out over toward my living room.

Lilah, the youngest, is cutting an apple pie into slices and placing them on plates. Not saying much of anything.

Brianna, a year younger than me, stands next to me, hands on her hips.

"That's Mark and Mary sitting together on the sofa. They live two houses down on the corner. Melissa is sitting on the hearth in front of the fireplace. Her husband Kevin is standing next to her. They live next to you on the other side. And the guy standing at the patio door looking out is Bert. He's the president of your Home Owner's Association."

I look at Brianna, my mouth open in awe. "How do you know this? Never mind." Brianna talks to everybody. She never meets a stranger. But even more important. "How do they even know about Thomas?"

"It was on the news," Lilah says, washing the knife.

"It was on the news?" I ask Brianna.

Their gazes land on me at once—startled, uncertain, as if I've just confessed something unthinkable.

"It's okay," Brianna says, pulling me into a hug. "You're okay."

Lilah puts the knife away and arranges the saucers of pie slices on a tray.

I groan when the doorbell rings. "Why so many people?"

"I'll get it," Brianna says. "Lilah. Give Audrey some pie."

"I'm not hungry," I say, but I sit down at the breakfast table, and take the fork Lilah hands me.

I'm still feeling groggy. Someone, Brianna I think, gave me something to help me sleep last night. I'd slept for… I glance at my watch… twelve hours. I never sleep that long.

After distributing the pie to my guests, which makes absolutely no sense to me, Lilah sits down next to me with her own piece of pie.

"It's good, huh?" Lilah asks as she takes a bite. Lilah never eats sweets. Things must be really bad for Lilah to eat pie.

"Yes." Surprisingly so. "Who made it?"

"HEB I think. I don't know who brought it."

Brianna comes back from answering the front door with a man wearing a suit in tow.

I glance at him out of the corner of my eye, then take another bite of pie. I have a good case of not caring. Learning that one's husband was killed in an airplane crash will do that to a person.

"This is Andrew Harrington," Brianna says, then lowers her voice. "Your attorney."

Alarmed, I look up at Andrew Harrington. "I have an attorney?"

He holds out a hand. "I'm Andrew," he says, kindly.

I set my fork down and put my hand in his.

"Is there someplace we can talk?" he asks. "In private."

"Lilah, get Mr. Harrington some pie, would you?" She turns back to Andrew. "Give me ten minutes and I'll have everyone out of here."

Andrew sits down across from me and dutifully eats the slice of pie Lilah puts in front of him.

Brianna takes the empty tray back into the living room.

"Thank y'all so much for coming," she says in what I recognize as her sweetest voice. "But we're gonna need a bit of privacy now."

Five minutes later she has my five unwanted guests herded out the door.

"We can talk now," she tells Andrew as she sits down at the table.

With Lilah on one side of me and Brianna on the other, I brace myself to hear what the attorney I didn't know I had has to say.

CHAPTER

THREE

Audrey

"I'VE GONE OVER ALL the paperwork," Andrew Harrington, Attorney says, taking a pair of wire-rimmed glasses out of his pocket and putting them on.

With the pie cleared away, I sit with my hands in my lap, watching him with heavy eyes.

He seems like a kind man. He has kind eyes and his tone is soft and understanding. Even so, it doesn't do much to keep the lump in my throat at bay.

The single word *widow* keeps swirling through my head. I'm too young to be a widow.

"I'm sorry," Brianna says glancing over at me. "Would you repeat that?"

"Sorry," I say, under my breath. My sister somehow knew my attention had wandered.

"Sure," Andrew says, looking into my eyes.

"Thomas made me executor of your estate, so I consulted with your accountant. I can skip over some of the details for now, but let me just boil it down.

"I'm afraid you're going to have to sell the house."

I blink at him. "Okay." Last night when the thought of living out here in Katy by myself crossed my mind, I'd shut it down. It wasn't something I could wrap my head around. But here he was bringing it up.

"You're okay with that?" Andrew asks.

"She needs to think about it," Brianna says.

"No," I say. "I don't need to think about it. I'm okay with it."

"Good," Andrew says. "That's good."

"So she'll have money, right?" Brianna asks. "From the sale of the house and insurance. She'll have insurance to start over, right?"

Frowning, Andrew rubs a hand over his face and removes his reading glasses.

"I regret to tell you the insurance is already allocated," he says.

"Already allocated?" Brianna says. "For what?"

"Thomas had some debt. Some rather large debts and even larger obligations."

Brianna looks at me. "What kind of debts did Thomas have?"

"I don't know. I didn't know he had any debts." I look outside at the mimosa tree Thomas had planted. He'd been so proud of himself when he'd dug that hole all by himself and dropped the five-foot tall tree we'd hauled from Home Depot into it.

"What kind of debts?" I ask Andrew.

"He had some pretty significant credit card debt, another mortgage, and—"

"Wait." Brianna holds up a hand. "Another mortgage?"

Andrew glances at me. Sits up a little straighter. "He has a condo in downtown Houston."

"Since when?" I ask. Thomas had never told me about him having another condo. When we'd met, he'd lived in an apartment near the Galleria.

"We can come back to those details."

"No. The condo is a mistake. There's no condo." I feel a little dizzy. A little faint. If there was a condo, I should know about it.

"Five years. It's not a mistake."

I steel myself for the sudden realization that I hardly knew Thomas at all. "Tell me why. Why did Thomas have a condo he never told me about?"

Neither one of my sisters says anything as I wait for Andrew to tell us these things about my husband. Things I hadn't known. Things I should have known.

"The child," Andrew says. "Thomas has a child."

I squeeze my eyes closed and Brianna grips my hand.

Lilah watches us all closely, then turns on Andrew. "You came all the way out here just to tell her this?" I hear the anger in Lilah's voice.

"It's okay, Lilah," I say, looking at her.

"No. It's not okay." She pins her gaze on Andrew. "If you don't have something good to tell Audrey, you can go. Can't you see she's already devastated?"

"I'm so sorry," Andrew says. "But I do have good news."

All three of us just look at him. A gust of warm Texas wind flutters a branch of the mimosa tree against the window.

"His grandfather left him a cabin. It's just outside a small town in the Colorado mountains."

"Who does that go to?" Brianna asks with obvious ire in her tone.

"It's protected. According to the grandfather's will, in the event that something happens to Thomas, it specifically goes to Thomas's first wife."

"Am I his first wife?" I ask, my voice sounding small. I no longer trust anything I thought I knew about my marriage.

Thomas has a child. A child with someone else. He'd never told me about having a child.

"Yes," Andrew says. "You're his first wife."

"The cabin is free and clear of any debts." He clears his throat. "There's a stipend that comes with it."

"So I own a house in Colorado?"

"Yes. Sort of. It's in a trust. It's yours but you have to live in it. You have to live in the house for one year for it to be yours. As long as you live there, you get the stipend that comes with it. But you can never sell the house."

"Thomas said we'd go to Colorado one day. I thought he meant we'd go there for a vacation."

"Audrey can't just move off to Colorado," Brianna says. "She has a job here. A life. Family."

"The cabin is paid for?" Lilah asks.

"Free and clear. All expenses paid by an executor."

"It must be a dump," Brianna says. "She can't live in a dump."

"It's not a dump," Andrew says.

"You've seen it?" Lilah asks, pinning Andrew with her gaze.

"No. But I've seen photos."

"Who's the executor?" I ask.

"I am," Andrew says.

Brianna sits back and crosses her arms. "It sounds fishy to me."

"What town?" I ask. "What town in Colorado?"

"Whiskey Springs."

Whiskey Springs. I'll think about it. Maybe something will come to me. A conversation. A mention.

But I know it won't. Just like the child. Apparently Andrew was a vault when it came to his personal life.

"How much is the stipend?" Lilah asks.

"The stipend is one million dollars."

"In lieu of millions of dollars in insurance," Brianna says, through gritted teeth. "The wife gets stuck with a cabin in the middle of nowhere and a million dollars. It won't last anytime." She looks at me. "You should contest the will."

"He has a child," I say. I don't even know who's side I'm on at this point. I'm just numb. Trying to hold all this information in my groggy brain and process it.

"So? He should have told you."

"And he shouldn't have died," I say. What I don't say is I shouldn't be a widow. I should not be a widow at twenty-seven.

"Ladies," Andrew says. "I'm going to leave some papers for you to look over. I'd like to come back in a couple of days after you've had some time to absorb everything."

My sisters glare at him.

"Okay," I say. "I need time to think about everything. And right now I'm very tired."

"I understand. I hate to be the one to drop all this on you. But..." He pulls a stack of papers from the briefcase at his feet. "There's one thing I think I need to clarify."

"Okay."

"The stipend. There's enough money in the account to

last all of your lifetimes put together and it's in an account that compounds daily." He leans forward, his gaze locked on mine. "The stipend will be deposited in your account the day you sign the papers. One million dollars. Every year. In perpetuity."

CHAPTER

FOUR

Audrey

"SHE CAN'T GO," Brianna says.

"She can't not go," Lilah says.

The three of us sit in my living room on the big sectional with nothing but the flames from the fireplace for light. The contract papers are scattered in front of us on the coffee table. Already dog-eared and highlighted.

It's dark now. After Andrew had left, I'd gone upstairs to take a nap. It seems like I can't get enough sleep.

Without reading it, I left the paperwork with my sisters to examine. And they had. I'll read it all later. Tomorrow maybe.

They'd gone through everything line by line. Brianna worked for an attorney for a year so she'd felt qualified to go through the paperwork line by line. Then she and Lilah had discussed it while I slept.

They'd even sent it over to our Uncle Carl. Uncle Carl is an attorney.

After I'd gotten up, they'd had pizza delivered of which I'd eaten all of one slice.

Not content with me eating just one slice of pizza, Lilah had made popcorn and set it out. I grab a handful and nibble on it.

"Audrey doesn't know anything about the mountains."

"How much different can it be than Katy?" Lilah, obviously not a fan of Katy, wrinkles her nose and picks up a bowl of popcorn. She doesn't eat sweets, but she'll eat anything salty. All ninety-five pounds of her.

"Have you ever been in the mountains?"

"She'll be fine. It's not just a cabin. It's a big house and it has maid service."

"I don't trust it." Brianna sits back and crosses her arms.

"You do know I'm right here," I say.

They both turn and look at me. I honestly think they had forgotten I was sitting right here.

"Of course we do," Brianna says.

"Is that in the contract?" I ask. "The maid service?"

"Yes," Lilah says, her face brightening. "We pulled up pictures on the Internet. Do you want to see them?"

"Sure." I shrug. I'm curious. For a lot of reasons. Not the least of which is why Lilah is suddenly fighting against Brianna for me to go to the cabin.

She links her phone to the big screen television—one of Thomas's prized possessions—on the wall over the fireplace and pulls up Google Earth. Types in the address.

"I see a lot of trees." Squinting, I lean forward. "And a rooftop. I can't tell anything about it."

"See," Brianna says. "It's blocked or something."

"It might be blocked," I say, munching on popcorn. "Some private residences are."

"You're both missing the point," Lilah says. "It's big. It's not just a cabin."

"Andrew said he has pictures. Did you ask him to send them over?"

They both look blankly at me. Then they look at each other.

I locate his business card on the coffee table and send him a text asking for pictures.

"Now," I say. "We just wait. He'll send..."

My phone vibrates.

"He must have been waiting."

"You have photos?" Lilah asks. "Put them up on the television."

I have three photographs. The first one is of the outside of the house.

"It looks like a lodge," Brianna says. "Two stories."

"Three if you count the attic." Lilac stands up to move closer to the television. "Look how pretty it is. It looks a log cabin but with glass. Look at all the windows. "

"We don't know how old the photos are," Brianna says.

Lilah turns on her. "Since when did you become so negative?"

"Since my sister is thinking about moving to the other side of the world to live."

"It's not the other side of the world," I say, keeping my eyes on the photo. Taking in the what is supposed to be a cabin, but looks more like a lodge just as Brianna pointed out.

"Couldn't be much worse than Katy," Lilah grumbles.

I don't say anything, but I tend to agree with Lilah. Something about the place looks so peaceful.

"Thomas never said anything to you about it?" Lilah asks.

I shake my head and lower my gaze to my phone.

"Lilah," Brianna admonishes.

"It's okay. We have to talk about him eventually." I slide to the next photo.

The inside of the cabin looks surprisingly modern with lots of light. An open floorplan much like this house.

"Look at that view," Lilah says. "You can sit in your living room and look out at the mountains."

"If she goes," Brianna says.

"I wonder if it's furnished," I say.

"It is. Fully furnished."

"That might not be the same furniture it has now."

"Brianna. Stop it."

"It doesn't matter," I say. "I don't need a lot. And with the stipend if I don't like it, I can replace it." I slide to the next photo.

"Look at that fireplace," Lilah says. "I think that's real wood."

Brianna bites her tongue.

"I can learn how to light a real fire," I say, knowing what Brianna is thinking. "How hard can it be?"

No one says anything for long enough that I shift my gaze to Lilah, then Brianna.

"You lost," Lilah says to Brianna.

"I know."

"Lost what?"

"The bet. I bet that you would be. Brianna bet that you wouldn't. I won."

"I haven't decided yet."

"You can't not go," Lilah says.

"She can live with me," Brianna offers.

"In your one-bedroom apartment? No thank you."

"Our parents."

I'm already shaking my head. "I'm definitely not moving back to Atlanta."

"By the way," Brianna says. "Our parents will be here in the morning."

"They should have just driven," Lilah says. "They'd be here by now."

"It's too hard on them. They're too old."

"They didn't have to come," I say. But I knew they'd be here for the funeral.

"It'll be good," Brianna says. "They can help pack."

"So they're too old to drive, but not too old to help pack?"

Brianna shrugs.

"Again. No need. I'm going to pack up my personal things and let the rest go with the house." I look up at the photo on the television. "It looks like my next place has everything I need."

Lilah is right.

I'm going.

Moving to Katy hadn't been my idea, but I'd gone along with it.

And Thomas had left everything to a child I hadn't even known he had.

And he might not even have known about it or intended it, but he'd left me a cabin in the mountains. Along with a healthy stipend.

I'm not going to let this opportunity slip by me.

Bradley Winslow

I FILL a mug with hot coffee, black, and take it outside with me. My dog, Biscuit, follows along at my heels.

Biscuit is a solid black lab that just showed up at my door one day. He was just a puppy. Probably ran off or someone ran him off. That was a year ago. Even now he's still pretty much a gangly puppy.

Sitting in one of the two wooden chairs on my deck, I stretch out my long legs, crossing them at the ankles, and take my first sip. The first sip always reminds me of drinking motor oil. Not that I've ever actually tasted motor oil. But if I did, I have little doubt there would be a resemblance.

My breath sends up a plume of smoke into the icy air and I set the mug on the little side table next to me to shove my hands in my warm pockets.

Biscuit lies down at my feet and tucks his head beneath his front paws.

The view from my deck couldn't be more perfect.

The cabin is remote by any standards. Five miles from the little town of Whiskey Springs, nestled high in the mountains along a winding mountain road. Technically not the end of the road, but the end of the road for all intents and purposes. It's been years since anyone lived in the cabin higher in the mountains. About once a week, a couple of women drive up and do whatever they do to check on it.

The snow-capped peaks, high above the tree line makes a wall to my west giving me an early sunset. The magnificence of it makes the early loss of daylight more than worth it.

Sloping down from my cabin, is a blanket of blue wildflowers stopping at the edge of little bubbling stream. The stream is currently swollen with snow melt.

A little doe stops at the edge of the stream, twitches her ears, then bends her neck for a drink of water.

A sure sign of spring. Already June. A late spring this year.

It's going to be a mild summer. We're going to need a lot of firewood for the cabins. More than usual.

That won't be a problem. My brother Wyatt is already on it. I heard the crack of his axe drifting through the valley just yesterday. Wyatt is old school. We have equipment, but Wyatt likes to heave the axe. I don't know if it's to keep himself in shape or to get out frustrations or to feel connected to our grandpa who chopped everything by hand in his day. Probably a little of all of the above.

Wispy clouds are drawn to the mountain peaks as early morning mist rises from the spruce and aspen and pine trees.

Today I've got to do some work in the Bentley cabin. Some major updating actually. My family owns thirty-seven cabins in and around Whiskey Springs at last count. One of those cabins, this one, I claimed for myself. My two brothers each claimed one for themselves, too. The other thirty-four are for tourists. Our busiest seasons are summer, of course, and oddly enough Christmas. People flock to Whiskey Springs for the trails and quiet serenity in the summers and the town's holiday festivities in December.

Our grandpa was a descendant of one of the first settlers of Whiskey Springs and he'd turned out to be a real estate mogul in his own right.

Somewhere along the way, someone had started naming the cabins by whoever they were bought from. So the Bentley cabin was one my father purchased from the Bentley family.

On occasion we'll flip one of the cabins when one of the tourists falls in love with it and wants to buy it. We don't have a problem with that. About once a year, my brothers and I will find a nice spot and build a cabin from the ground up. Another tradition started by Grandpa. That man had more energy than anybody these days. They don't make them like that anymore.

We usually name the new cabins after the first person who rents them out or we name them after a pet. Or whatever seems to fit.

Last year, I'd started calling one Aspen Grove because it sat right smack in the middle of grove of aspen trees and the name had stuck.

Picking up my mug, the coffee cooled enough now to drink, I look to the east.

Misty tendrils drift up from the trees in that direction, too.

But then I smell it. Chimney smoke. I didn't light a fire in my fireplace this morning. Not enough time to enjoy it. But I know chimney smoke when I smell it.

I stand up and walk to the edge of my deck, put my hands on the rough wooden railing and lean over to get a better look. Biscuit jumps up and goes with me, ready for any adventure.

I pull my phone out of my pocket and dial my brother Caleb's number.

"Hey," I say. "Heard any rumors about anyone staying up at the Albright place?"

"Good morning to you, too," Caleb says.

"Sorry if my level of morning chipperness isn't up to your standards. But have you?"

"No. But it's not our cabin, so I might not hear about it."

"If we bought it, we could keep an eye on it."

"If they would sell it, we would buy it. You just don't like anyone close by."

"Probably kids again. I'll head up in a bit and run them off."

"Want me to call the sheriff?"

"No need. I'm perfectly capable of running people off on my own."

"I have no doubt about that."

"See you at Mom and Dad's tonight to go over plans for this year's cabin?"

"Wouldn't miss it."

I disconnect the line and slide my phone back into my pocket. With the shift in the wind, I can definitely see smoke coming from the Albright chimney. Doesn't look like anything to be alarmed about. Just smoke from a fireplace. It has three of them.

Technically it's not a cabin. Technically it's a manor. A house more suited to Vail or one of the larger, more affluent towns. Unfortunately, it's been neglected and left to run down. Probably been a good ten years since anyone lived in it. A house has to be lived in or it dies. Strange but true fact. I've seen it one too many times. I've also watched houses come back to life with a good dose of updates and care.

Maybe it's time we make another run at the Albright family about buying it. We can focus on the dangers of having squatters and campers in there.

Last time we checked, it was owned by a city fellow named Thomas Albright. He wouldn't even talk to us about selling. Seemed convinced that he'd be using it someday. And maybe he will. I hope so for the house's sake.

No reason to hurry. The trespassers aren't going anywhere anytime soon. If I've seen it once, I've seen it a hundred times.

"Ready to go to work, Biscuit?" I ask.

Biscuit stands up and barks once. I take that as a yes.

I gulp down the rest of my coffee/motor oil and go inside to get ready to head out to the Bentley cabin after a quick stop by the Albright place to suggest whoever is homesteading there find a legitimate cabin to rent.

We certainly have enough of them to choose from. If they can't afford one of the cabins—a lot of people can't —they can throw up a tent at one of our two camp-grounds. Thirty dollars a night will get a person a tent and a spot to pitch it on. If they're nice, we'll even throw in a bundle of firewood. We cater to people from all walks of life.

Young people might start off in tents, then come back a few years later as gainfully employed adults with kids of their own.

Sometimes we have to play the long game.

CHAPTER
SIX

Audrey

THE OLD FELLOW down at the General Store in Whiskey Springs had thrown in a bundle of kindling to go along with everything else I'd bought. He'd been free with his suggestions, especially after he learned I was headed up to the Albright place.

He'd even helped me load the bundle of firewood on the floorboard in the front seat of my car. It had been the only place left to put anything after I'd packed in all the groceries.

Even though I'd seen pictures, all of three, I'd had absolutely no idea what to expect, but with my house in

Katy up for sale, I'd brought a lot of my personal items with me. I brought about half my clothes and would have brought more, but my sister Brianna had convinced me to at least check out the house first. To see if it was livable. Before I had my books and kitchenware shipped.

I hadn't been worried. I'd believed in the photographs I'd seen. What I hadn't counted on was how welcoming the house felt. How much like home.

Now that I have the fire in the fireplace going, I don't want it to go out, so I shove another log in there and poke at them with the poker.

Our fireplace in Katy had been gas, so burning actual wood is a new experience. We hadn't had a fireplace of any kind in our house in Atlanta where we'd grown up. As such, a fireplace is one of my favorite things to have in a house.

Satisfied that my fire is going to hold for a bit, I dust off my hands and walk around the big open area that encompasses the living room, dining room, kitchen, and a little study. When I'd gotten here last night, I'd been too tired to do much more than collapse on the sofa and sleep.

I promised both my sisters I'd FaceTime them this morning so they could see for themselves that I was in a safe place and not a hovel. It was definitely the opposite of a hovel.

Not even being the oldest of three could get me out of that. They were all worried about me.

And maybe they had good reason to.

A twenty-seven-year-old widow is someone to worry about to begin and end with without adding on the strange house in the strange place.

The house in Katy hadn't been mine to keep even if I wanted to. Thomas had bought it with such a huge mortgage, there was no way I could have kept it even if it had been an option. And that didn't even include the HOA, the taxes, and maintenance.

I honestly hadn't even realized how high we'd been living. My little salary at the art gallery wouldn't even have touched the expenses.

And then there was his debt. His insurance went to pay off his debt. I hadn't known about that either.

But the kicker of it all had been finding out that my husband had a child with another woman. A secret baby. And he took care of them. He paid the mortgage on a condo for them in downtown Houston.

No one gave me any kind of explanation, but I have a theory. My theory is that Thomas wanted us to live in Katy to keep me as far away from his baby mama as possible. It must have driven him crazy that I worked in a gallery downtown. Not that he and the mother of his child would have known each other even if we'd talked.

If I was right, he planned on us never meeting and we never will. If she was at the funeral, I would have no way of knowing. There were a lot of people from his work I didn't know and she could easily have been one of those many people I hadn't recognized.

My sisters and parents had kept me close and guarded during the entire funeral and the wake that followed.

But there had been one bright spot in Thomas's estate. This mountain cabin just outside Whiskey Springs, Colorado.

Somehow it was protected from whatever financial disaster Thomas's life had been. Apparently, Thomas's grandfather had passed after Thomas had his illegitimate child. He must have known about it and made sure the cabin was protected.

The attorney had tried to explain it, but I hadn't even pretended to understand. All I knew was that this mountain cabin now belongs to me. All I have to do is live in it.

A cabin bigger than our house in Katy, so technically not a cabin. Technically a house. A house that's going to take a lot of upkeep.

My sister Brianna calls me first.

"Good morning," she says with her usual morning chipperness.

"Remember," I say, grumbling a bit. "It's an hour later for you."

"Have you had coffee?" she asks.

"I have."

"Good. Then show me around."

"Don't tell Lilah," I say. "I'm supposed to show her first."

"It's what she gets for being a sleepyhead. Just give me a tour already."

I flip the camera and start with the fire in the fireplace.

"It looks kind of big," Brianna says. "I hope it's not shooting flames out the chimney."

"Really? It looks good to me."

"If you burn the house down, you'll have to move back here."

"Duly noted. I'll let it die down some."

"The furniture looks okay," Brianna says. "Does it smell old?"

"Actually no. Someone's been keeping it freshened up. It smells a little bit like… cinnamon. And vanilla."

"It looks like it would smell like wood and old leather."

"It does. All of those things. It's hard to explain."

"Nice couch," she says.

"This big couch is comfortable for sleeping," I tell her.

"You slept on it. Why?"

"Too tired to do anything else."

"I see your luggage sitting there by the stairs. You have a lot to do. I should have come with you."

"You have work. And besides, I needed to do this."

I take her from the living room, past the heavy dining room table with six heavy wooden chairs, into the kitchen.

"Everything looks new in here." I run a hand over the

cast iron burners on the gas stovetop. "Look at the size of this refrigerator." The whole thing, a side by side refrigerator and freezer is twice as big as a normal appliance.

I open the door where I have the things I'd bought yesterday at the General Store. A half-gallon of milk. A dozen eggs. Some fruit and vegetables. "I don't think it's ever been used."

"I'm surprised they didn't stock it for you."

"There's water," I say. "That was already here."

"That was nice of them."

I ignore the sarcasm in her tone. "I have to figure out how to use this coffee maker. I just made instant this morning."

"You made instant coffee when you have that fancy machine sitting on the cabinet."

"I have to learn how to use it. And yes. If you'd come with me, you would have figured it out already."

"Let's go upstairs. See your bedroom. Then I want to go out on the back deck."

"How do you know there's a deck?"

"I see it through the windows."

"Good eyes."

I take her up the wide sweeping stairs. "There are three bedrooms. Maybe four. I have to decide which one I'm going to take."

"Take the primary."

"When I figure out which one that is. They're all huge with huge bathrooms."

"It looks kind of like a lodge, doesn't it?"

"It kind of does. I wonder about the history of it."

"You'll find out if you go into town any. People like to talk."

"You'll definitely find out when you get here."

"I'll make it my mission."

I show her the three bedrooms. All with big walk in closets and ensuite bathrooms. I show her the views from all three.

"They all have great views," she says.

"I think that was by design."

"Which one are you leaning towards?"

"I don't know. I think—Oh." I look at my phone. "Lilah's calling. Let me talk to her. I promised."

"It's okay. We'll talk soon."

I switch over to Lilah's call. "Hey Lilah."

"Hey. Are you ready to give me a tour?"

"I'm upstairs so we'll start here."

I give my youngest sister a similar tour of the house in reverse.

I haven't even chosen my bedroom yet and already it's starting to feel like home.

As I talk to Lilah, I notice that one of the bedrooms has a fireplace in it.

And I decide right then and there. That one's mine.

"I'm taking this bedroom with the fireplace," I tell Lilah. "You and Brianna can fight over the other two bedrooms when you get here."

"I can't wait," Lilah says. "You should have let me come with you."

"I know. And it would have been a whole lot easier to have you and Brianna with me, but I needed to do it by myself."

It was going to take me a while to process everything that had happened since Thomas's plane crash. To figure out what my next step is.

I've taken the first one by coming here. Having a million dollars sitting in my account certainly made that first step easier.

I check it a couple of time a day to make sure it doesn't disappear. That they don't take it back.

I find it hard to believe that there's a trust that just gives me money. I get them giving me the house. But the money is going to take some getting used to.

Sometimes I want to talk to Thomas so badly it takes me to my knees.

But then I just imagine him flying in his airplane. I like to think of him flying, a place where he was happiest. It helps with the pain. Doesn't help much with the shock. But that will get better with time.

At least that's what they tell me.

"What's that noise?" Lilah asks. "Doorbell?"

I stand at the front windows and look out toward the circle drive at the front of the house. "There's someone here. A pickup truck."

"Find out who it is before you answer the door," Lilah says.

"Lilah. I'm going to go now. I have a visitor. Love you. Bye."

Blowing out a breath of frustration, I disconnect the line and slide my phone into the back pocket of my jeans.

It's a small town. People are going to be curious.

My sisters have to get used to it. As do I.

I square my shoulders and open the door.

CHAPTER

SEVEN

Bradley

IT'S BEEN AWHILE since I've been to the Albright place. It's a big house. Only four bedrooms, but if memory serves, all the rooms are oversized giving it a spacious feel.

Getting out of my truck, I can't help but notice the smoke billowing out of the living room chimney. Someone has a big fire going. Maybe too big.

Being part of the volunteer fire department, I'm always on the lookout for people doing things that aren't in their best interests.

Someone left pots of colorful flowers on the front porch. Blue butterfly begonias. White petunias. Salmon-colored geraniums. All fluttering in the breeze. A bumblebee buzzing from one to the other. Maybe the Albrights decided to rent the place out. Or... maybe that city fellow decided to come up for the summer.

A young lady, mid to late twenties, answers the door.

First impression. Pretty. But her eyes are haunted. And she's thin as a rail.

A city girl. I can always spot them. Brown hair with intentional blonde streaks pulled back in a messy ponytail.

Not squatters. Not squatters or kids.

"Do you always open the door to strangers?" I ask.

"No... I..." Looking confused, she leans against the door, one hand still on the knob. "I thought..."

"It's okay," I say, easing my expression into a more welcoming smile. "I'm your neighbor. First house down the way. You might have noticed when you drove in."

"I didn't really pay much attention," she says, twisting the doorknob. "Sorry."

"It's okay. My place is kind of hidden back in the trees."

She nods. Then seems to realize she's not being neighborly. "Do you want to come in?"

"I don't want to interrupt."

"You're not interrupting." She looks past me now toward my truck. "You have a dog in your truck."

"Yeah. That's Biscuit."

"He can come in, too."

I open my mouth to tell her that Biscuit is the kind of dog a person should get to know before he comes for a visit, but something, that hauntedness in her eyes perhaps, changes my mind.

"Okay. I'll get him." As I walk back to the truck to get Biscuit, I consider that she looks like someone who could use the company of a dog.

Tail wagging and tongue hanging out, Biscuit jumps out of the truck and races up the porch stairs toward the door. I follow at a slower pace.

She kneels down and lets Biscuit lick her face while she pets him.

The smile on her face says it all.

"Do you two know each other?" I ask.

Standing up, she looks at me, confused again. "No. He's just so friendly."

"He was a stray when I got him," I explain. "I thought maybe he was yours."

"Oh. How long have you had him?" She steps back, giving us both space to come inside.

"About a year," I say, my gaze drawn to the blazing fire in the fireplace. "That's quite a fire you have going."

"Yeah." She runs a hand over her hair. "So I've been told."

"Do you have plenty of firewood?"

"I don't know. I just got here." She glances around. "I don't really know."

"Your husband?" I ask, knowing it's not really a question, but she's wearing a wedding ring, so it's sort of open-ended.

"No. I—"

Biscuit jumps onto the sofa in front of the fireplace, turns around three times, then lies down.

"Biscuit," I say, pointing to the floor.

"He's okay," she says. "I know your dog's name, but I don't know yours."

"Bradley Winslow. And you are…"

"Audrey Sinclair." She sits on the sofa next to Biscuit and scratches his head. I sit on the armchair next to them.

"What brings you to Whiskey Springs, Audrey Sinclair?"

"It's a long story," she says.

I don't have to know Audrey to know that she's not about to tell me that long story right now.

"Do you happen to know anything about coffee makers?" she asks.

"I might know a thing or two," I say, trying to hide my relief that we're done with the small talk. "How can I help?"

CHAPTER
EIGHT

Audrey

I TOOK a page out of Brianna's playbook and used diversion to get my new neighbor's attention off of me and my reason for being here.

He had a good point about me opening the door for strangers. But he'd looked like a regular guy. Unlike me, he looks like he belongs here in Whiskey Springs. Jeans. Worn work boots. A blue and green flannel shirt rolled up at the wrists. A white t-shirt beneath it.

Standing up, he lifts his baseball cap, runs a hand through short dark brown hair and settles it back on his head.

And he has a dog.

What's not to like?

"Whoa," he says, looking from my three suitcases to me. "You need some help getting those upstairs?"

"I wouldn't turn it down. I got them this far."

"Let me just…" He picks up two of them. Carries them to the top of the stairs like they're weightless, then comes back down for the third.

"Anything else you need me to take up?"

"That's it for right now. Thanks."

"All you had to do was ask."

Obviously I hadn't actually had to ask.

As he fiddles with the fancy coffeemaker on my counter. I find a bag of coffee beans—not expired in the pantry and pull the carton of milk I'd bought in town, from the refrigerator.

"Do you know how it works?" I ask.

"My brother actually has one similar to it. So. Yeah."

"Oh. Okay." I take two mugs out of the cabinet. Then on second thought I wash them before handing them to him. Even though everything looks clean, I really don't know if it is.

To be on the safe side, I'll run everything through the dishwasher after he leaves.

By the time I get the mugs washed, the scent of freshly brewed coffee fills the air.

"It smells like a coffee shop in here," I say.

"I usually drink motor oil."

"What?"

"Nothing. I just don't usually take the time to make good coffee. And besides I don't have one of these fancy machines at my place."

I study Bradley Winslow. He's tall. About six feet. Dark hair. A little uneven on the ends that barely brush his collar.

I reflexively compare him to Thomas. Thomas always had a perfect haircut. Cut every two weeks whether he needed it or not.

Would Thomas have known how to work this coffee maker? I'm thinking not. I'm thinking he would have found his way downtown to the coffee shop. Probably would have gotten up early and come back with two cups of coffee.

And yet he was a pilot. He could have figured it out. If he wanted to.

"Audrey?" Bradley asks.

I blink and realize he must have been talking to me.

"I'm sorry. I was thinking about something else." I do it all the time. My family is used to it and it doesn't bother them, but he's looking at me like something's wrong with me.

"I was just asking how much milk you like in your coffee."

"Oh," I say. "Enough so it doesn't take like coffee. Or

motor oil." Geez. I'm not fit to be around other people. Brianna and Lilah were right. I should have brought them.

Bradley gives me a little grin, then as he makes the coffee, I twist at my wedding ring.

He'd asked about my husband. People are going to ask. I'm going to have to tell them. There's no way around it.

Bradley hands me a cup of hot coffee. I take it from him and set it on counter.

"You asked what brought me to Whiskey Springs."

"Just making conversation. You don't have to answer."

"This house belonged to my husband's grandfather."

"Theodore Albright."

"Yes. And now it apparently belongs to me."

Bradley sets his mug down, too. Leans a hip against the kitchen island and studies me.

"Last I heard it belonged to a fellow named Thomas Albright. He sold it to you?"

"No. I inherited it."

He tilts his head to the side and looks at me. "I'm a little confused now."

"Thomas Albright was my husband."

"Was." I can see him putting things together. *Was. Inherited.*

"I know it's confusing because I didn't take his name.

"Not unusual."

Apparently somehow word about Thomas's accident had not traveled to Whiskey Springs.

"Thomas Albright was killed in an airplane crash two weeks ago." I straighten my shoulders and force myself to follow through with the words. "I'm his widow."

CHAPTER
NINE

Bradley

I TAKE a sip of the coffee I'd just made and burn my tongue in the process.

I'm standing in the Albright kitchen talking to the widow of Thomas Albright. Granddaughter-in-law of Theodore Albright.

"Not only a long story," I say. "But a confusing one. And sad."

She smiles a little and takes a cautious sip of her coffee. "You have no idea."

"I'm sorry for your loss."

"Thank you. I never know how to respond when

someone says that." She slips onto one of the barstools and I walk around to sit next to her.

"I don't think you really have to respond."

"Good," she says. "That's good."

"And just for the record, I don't think you have to tell people either."

"It's a small town. People are going to want to know."

"Only because they're nosy and don't have a life of their own. No one needs to know why you're here." I know she's right, but I feel instinctively protective toward her.

"I guess they'll find out anyway."

"They will. People have a way of finding out things about other people. Human nature."

She picks up her coffee mug and stares into it. Now I understand why she'd drifted off a few minutes ago.

"So... are you just visiting or are you planning on living out here?"

"I was thinking I'd live here," she says, still looking into her coffee as though she would find answers there. "It's either that or go back to live with my parents in Atlanta or live with one of my sisters in Houston."

"Do you have children?"

"No." Biscuit wanders over and nudges her hand for a pet. "No pets either."

"So it's just you. Up here. Alone."

"I have neighbors," she says, looking up to meet my gaze, a little smile playing about her lips. That little smile doesn't do anything to take away the hauntedness from her eyes though.

"You have one neighbor and I'm a mile away. It's nothing like Atlanta or Houston."

"Maybe that's a good thing."

"Maybe. What do you do?"

"Right now? I don't do anything. I worked for an art gallery in Houston. But... I didn't want to go back to it."

"I'm sure you have your reasons."

"Yeah." She blows out a breath. "Actually. I'm planning to take my time. Figure out what I want to do next."

"Sounds like a good plan."

I take a business card out of my wallet and slide it over to her. "If you need anything at all. Call me. That's my cell phone number."

She picks up my card. "Timber Ridge Cabins and Timber Company. Vice President."

"Yes. Well. It's a family business, so I'm not sure how much clout is behind that title."

She looks at me with her shadowed green eyes. I'd been right. I definitely understand now why she has that haunted look about her. Widowed for just two weeks. Still trying to get the ground back beneath her feet.

"Maybe it doesn't have a lot of clout now," she says. "But it will one day. It's you and your three brothers?"

"Yes. And our parents."

She turns my card over, end over end. "You've always lived here in Whiskey Springs?"

"I moved away when I went to college, but it was expected that I'd come back and help with the family business."

She nods. "Do you like it?"

"Sure. I like it okay."

"Just okay? There's something else that you dream about doing?"

"No. I can't say that there is. Not work wise anyway."

There are plenty of things I think about. Like getting married and having a couple of kids. But that's not the kind of thing to walk in a stranger's—a widow at that—house and say.

"Good. If there is, you should go ahead and do it. Don't wait."

"Speaking of work," I say, standing up. "I've got quite a bit of work to do on the Bentley cabin."

She stands up, too. "Thanks for making the coffee."

"Sure thing. Call me. I'll come back and teach you how to use it."

"Okay. I'll do that."

I have a feeling she won't call me. But I'll come back by. Maybe in the morning. Show her how it's done.

I have a feeling Audrey Sinclair is going to need a lot of protecting out here. And that same feeling tells me I'm the man to protect her.

CHAPTER
TEN

Audrey

I TAKE my cup of coffee, as good as any designer coffee, and sit in front of my fireplace with the big flames. They're starting to die down now and I resist the temptation to toss another log in there.

There are only a few more logs left from my shopping trip at the General Store. I need to take a look around to see if there is any more firewood already here. I hadn't thought to look until Bradley had ask me how much I had.

Speaking of Bradley, I'd done exactly what I'd said I wasn't going to do. I'd given him my whole life history.

He knew everything now. He knew where my parents live. Where my sisters live. That I have sisters.

He knows that I'm a widow and that I now own the house. It might be in a trust, but according to my uncle, the house is mine and there is nothing anyone including the baby mama and child can ever do about it.

Just like there was nothing I could do about Thomas's life insurance going to them. It's how they had set it up. Thomas and his grandfather. Independently it seems. What wife would think to ask her new husband if his life insurance was going to her or to another woman and child?

So now Bradley Winslow knows all about me and all I know about him is that he lives down the road and works in his family business.

I'd gone from not talking about Thomas and the whole situation to spilling it all to Bradley.

It's not entirely my fault. I blame his eyes. Bradley's kind eyes. His dog didn't help. Apparently I'm a sucker for a guy with kind eyes especially if he has a dog.

I pull his card out of my pocket and read over it again. Then enter his number in my phone contacts.

Timber Ridge Cabins.

A quick google search sends me to their website. They own upwards of three dozen cabins in town and supply all the town's firewood from their tree farm. They also provide Christmas trees for Whiskey Springs and the surrounding area.

Apparently the Winslows are a big name in the area.

Great. Now everyone around here will not only know that I'm here, but also why.

I guess if I was going to spill my guts to someone, it was only natural that I'd spill them to the guy with the kind blue eyes and adorable dog, not to mention whose family owns half the town.

Maybe it was simply that he's a stranger to me.

Talking about Thomas to someone I don't know is different from talking to someone who knew him.

I pause with my mug halfway to my lips.

What had I been thinking?

I'm sitting in Thomas's grandfather's house. Bradley would have known Theodore Albright.

He just hadn't known about me. Thomas and I hadn't been married all that long and Thomas had never told me about this place, much less brought me here.

So even though Bradley is a complete stranger to me, he's not a complete stranger to the Albright family.

When I screw something up, I do it right.

I need to talk to the attorneys. To see if it's okay for me to talk about the inheritance.

Bradley didn't seem to know anything about it.

Maybe I'll just be smart and keep it to myself from here on out.

Bradley didn't seem like the kind of guy who would gossip, but still... He is a product of a small town.

After finishing my coffee, I take my mug back to the

kitchen. Put it in the dishwasher along with Bradley's mug and all the other dishes I can fit in there and turn it on.

Turns out the house is well stocked. I don't even need to bring any of my own kitchenware. Everything here is nicer than anything I had anyway. That was saying something considering that Thomas bought designer everything.

Some of my things, however, are sentimental even if it's not as high quality. I'll have it sent up here, then sort through it and donate what I don't want to keep. Maybe donating things locally will help me make a place for myself here.

Sometimes it's the little things that make a big difference.

I've no more than walked out onto the back deck than Lilah calls me back.

Having protective sisters takes some getting used to, but there are worse things.

CHAPTER
ELEVEN

Bradley

I STOP by the General Store to pick up some supplies before I head up to the Bentley cabin.

"Headed to the Bentley Place?" John ask as he rings up my box of screws and half a dozen two-by-fours.

"Oh yeah. I'm sure I'll be back with an order of things I'm going to need. Just basically going up to assess. Take care of the most dangerous."

"Going to need new appliances from what I hear."

"You heard right."

"Just let me know. I can order whatever you need. Get it for you at cost."

"I'm counting on it."

An older fellow comes in through the front door. John waves and goes back to work tying the two by fours with a line of twine.

"You don't have to tie that up," I say. "I've got it."

"It's no trouble. I saw your new neighbor yesterday. Audrey."

"Did you now?"

"Yep. You want some varnish while you're here?"

"Not sure which color. I'll come back for it."

"Yeah. She didn't have much to say. Had to drag it out of her that she was headed up to the Albright place."

I don't think John is fishing for information. I think he's just making conversation. As such people tell him things. Not sure how much of that information he spreads.

"Didn't tell you why she's here?"

"Nope."

I hand him my credit card.

"She was a closed book. Got to admire that these days. My granddaughter could probably find out everything about on that intertube in about half a minute."

I chuckle. John's close enough to be in the right ballpark.

"I don't use it much either," I say. "But Cade's put up a website for us."

"You don't say? Maybe I'll get him to set one up for me."

"Couldn't hurt."

"Yeah. A lot of people are driving into Boulder and a lot more are ordering things and having them delivered. Seems like the world is changing. Getting too big for a little place like this.

"Not a chance." I tuck my credit card back into my wallet. "We need you here."

"One of the big chains was nosing around. If that happens, I'm out."

"I'm on the city council, John. They'll never get my vote."

"Unfortunately, there's other people on there besides you. People that want the big chains."

Hefting my lumber over my shoulder, I grab my box of nails. "We'll fight it if it happens. Until then, let's not buy trouble."

"Getting too old to fight," John says. "See you tomorrow."

"Probably," I say. "Oh. Can I get a bag of kindling? Put it on my tab?"

"What you buying kindling for? You know I bought it from you."

"It's a gift. And a show of good faith to make sure you keep the doors open."

John grumbles, but he grabs a bag of kindling and slips it into my paper sack.

"Don't forget to put it on my tab."

"Get out of here," John says. "I got work to do."

He won't put it on my tab. I already know.

But from what I've seen of Audrey's propensity to make super large fires in her fireplace, she's going to need it.

I'm just being neighborly.

It has nothing to do with her haunted green eyes in her elfin-like features.

Doesn't mean anything that I can't stop thinking about her.

TWELVE

Audrey

I sit on the deck, talking to Lilah, listening while she tells me about her plan. Lilah is an artist at heart who works at a bar to pay the bills.

"I'm saving my money," she tells me. "so I can buy art supplies and take two weeks off to come and visit you. I can paint while I'm there, right?"

"Of course you can, but Lilah?"

An acrobatic little chipmunk races along the wooden rails, hops onto a long-hanging maple tree limb with fresh spring buds, and vanishes.

"Just quit your job."

"I can't do that," she says. "The Millers need me. I've worked for them since I was in high school."

"And how old are you now?"

"Twenty-three."

I wait while she takes a minute to think about that.

"I know what you're saying," she says. "But I can't just move in on you."

"You're right," I say, watching a flock of black birds swoop down onto the ground below. Their sleek black feathers stand out in sharp contrast to the dewy spring grass and flowers in a blanket of light blue sweeping down the hillside. "So come up when you're ready. Take your two weeks and then we'll talk."

"Okay. But you said you needed some time. That we had to wait."

"When do you think you'll be ready?"

Lilah hesitates. "Two or three weeks. Maybe four. But I can come earlier if you want me to."

"Lilah. Stop worrying. Just come when you want to. I'm sure that by the time you're ready to come up here, I'll be more than ready to see you."

"Okay. So tell me about your neighbor."

"Just a run-of-the-mill neighbor. You know how I feel about neighbors."

"I don't think you like neighbors very much."

"Not really." Handsome blue-eyed ones might be okay.

"How did you put it? They think just because they live

nearby they have the right to just drop in anytime they want to."

"Something like that."

"You sound good," Lilah says. "I'm going to take a nap before I have to get ready for work. Call me if you need anything."

"I will. I think I'm going to take a nap, too."

"Good idea. I love you, Sis."

"Love you, too."

After I disconnect the line, I get up to go back inside. The back of the house is more impressive than the front of the house and that's saying a lot.

It's got so much glass, being inside is almost like being outside.

I'm a little excited to see snowfall on the deck, but that will be awhile. It's just now summer. According to all accounts, summer will bring cold nights and warm days, but snow is unlikely until September. Not impossible, but unlikely.

I'm wondering if I should wash the bedsheets before I take a nap as I go back inside.

I walk to the sink, fill a glass with water, then turn around to face the living room while I drink it.

That's when I see the vase of yellow daisies sitting on the kitchen island.

They were most definitely not there before.

They were not there when Bradley was here. He and I

had stood right here while he made coffee. There had been no flowers. No vase. No flowers.

Frozen in place, I glance about the room.

I don't see anything else out of the ordinary.

The flames have died down in the fireplace. That's about it.

Giving the flowers a wide berth, keeping one eye on them, I walk around to the front door. Check the locks.

Everything seems to be in order. I know no one went in the back door while I was outside. I would have seen them.

I stand at the large front window and watch the road. My house is at the end. Anyone coming this far is most definitely either coming to see me or is lost.

There's no dust like there had been earlier when Bradley drove off. Not even a light dusting in the air.

No sign that anyone was here.

But someone was here. Flowers don't just randomly appear out of nowhere.

Maybe Bradley had slipped back in and left the flowers while I was outside.

It would be a little bit strange, but...

Checking the door lock one more time, I go back to the kitchen island and slide the vase of flowers toward me.

Where would he even get flowers? Just happened to have a vase of flowers in his truck?

There's no card.

No indication of who they're from.

I send Bradley a text.

> Hi. This is Audrey. Your new neighbor. Did you see anyone head up this way as you were leaving?

He's going to think something's wrong with me, but I need to know. Mostly I need to know if he came back and left the flowers.

If he did, it's still strange, but it's a kind of strange I can grasp. The alternative... not so much.

BRADLEY

> No. I stopped by the General Store in town, then came straight here to the Bentley house. Didn't see anyone. Something wrong?

> No. Just thought I heard something. Sorry to bother.

BRADLEY

> Seriously. If you need something I can be right there.

> Thank you.

I examine the flowers. Dewy and fresh. Like they just came out of a flower shop. I take a photo of them and make a notation in my phone. If anything happens to me either one of my sisters can access my phone and maybe this photo will be a clue.

I'm imagining things.

Maybe they were here all along and they just somehow got slid over to the middle of the island.

Maybe it's the grief causing me to get confused. Grief, especially the kind that comes with trauma, can do that. I'd looked it up.

Not sleepy anymore. Definitely too on edge to sleep, I head upstairs to check out my bedroom and unpack.

As I walk upstairs, it occurs to me that I should get a dog. A big dog like Bradley has. A dog like Biscuit would bark and scare intruders away.

If I knew Bradley a little better, I'd ask him about the flowers. It would be good to have corroboration on something like that.

Trying to put the mystery of the flowers behind me for now—surely there's a logical explanation—I walk through my bedroom of choice and into the closet.

I'm delighted to see that it has a washer and dryer right there in the closet. What better place to have a washing machine than in the closet?

Unfortunately, when I open the lid of the washing machine, it smells vile. The dryer has pockets of rust. There's no way I'm going to put my clothes in either one of them.

Now I have a reason to call Bradley. To find out where to get a new washer and dryer.

And... I look around the closet... the closets in this house have most definitely been neglected. Unlike the kitchen, they don't look like they've ever been updated.

There is so much that can be done in here. Fortunately, I have some experience. This is going to be fun. It's been awhile since I felt that little unexpected spurt of anticipation.

I need some paper and a tape measure. I have a pad of paper in my computer bag, but no tape measure. It's not something I usually carry around, but if I'd thought it through I would have brought one. There's always something to measure in a new place.

It would be better to start with a blank slate in here. I need to pull down all the old uneven shelves and rusty metal rods and then I need to paint the walls.

I need paint.

Once it's painted, I can measure and start creating my own custom closet.

My hands tucked in my warm oversized sweatshirt, I wander around to the other two large bedrooms. They have similar closet situations. Same with the smaller bedroom.

I designed our closets in Katy, but I did that on a budget. I don't have a budget on these.

Nothing I like better than a project.

As I walk back downstairs to make myself some hot tea, I feel a little bit less sad than I have since that rainy Tuesday night when Thomas's plane had gone down and not only that, I'm feeling more optimistic than I have for a long time.

All at the prospect of designing my own closets from the ground up.

CHAPTER
THIRTEEN

Bradley

With a two-page list of nothing but basic supplies I need to get even started on the Bentley cabin, I lock up and head out. Biscuit jumps into the passenger seat and off we go.

My gaze lands on the bag of kindling I'd impulsively bought for Audrey and I check my messages to see if she texted again.

Nothing new, but something spooked her. She doesn't strike me as the kind of girl who would text a man she just met without a good reason.

Since she lives less than a mile from my cabin—actually I can cut through and walk to her cabin in fifteen minutes—it's a mile by road, I can just swing by and check on her.

It's what a good neighbor would do, especially now that I know what she's been through. Hell backwards. That's what it sounds like she's been through.

She hadn't said where she was actually from, and I'll google plane crashes when I get home, but she has a southern accent. I'm leaning toward Texas. Assuming I'm right and she's from Houston or even Atlanta, it took a lot of courage for her to come out here and by herself, too.

I can't even begin to speculate why she would have moved out here. Maybe she hadn't had a choice. Or maybe she wanted the adventure. Or maybe it was just what she told me. To take some time to figure out what she wanted to do next. I imagine that includes adjusting to being a single woman again.

Biscuit sits up and barks once as we turn into her circle drive.

Already the old house is starting to look like it has a little more life in it. Just knowing that someone is living here will do that.

I grab the bag of kindling and slide out of the truck, Biscuit right behind me.

Biscuit bounds up the steps in front of me. Audrey might deny it, but Biscuit seems to know her. Or maybe Biscuit just likes a pretty girl as much as I do. I can't blame him.

"Hi," she says, looking surprised. Her cheeks are flushed like maybe she just ran down the stairs to answer the door.

"Hi. I don't normally drop in on people like this, at least not twice a day, but your text message made me worry that you'd been a little spooked."

She takes a step back to give me and Biscuit space to come inside.

Biscuit looks like he's in love as she scratches his head.

"Biscuit," I say. "Have some dignity."

"He's okay. He reminds me of a dog I had when I was growing up."

"I see." It's sort of a connection. "So. Are you okay?"

"I was upstairs. Wishing for a tape measure."

"Ah. I missed it."

"Missed what?"

"I brought you kindling."

"Oh." There's that ghost of a smile again. "For the fireplace."

"Since you seem to enjoy the fires so much. But if I'd known, I would have brought you a tape measure. What are we measuring?"

"Closets." She takes the kindling. Sniffs it. Then searches my eyes. "I want to strip everything out of them. Everything. All the shelves and rods. Paint the walls. Maybe even new flooring. And design them from the ground up."

"Sounds like my kind of project."

"You do renovations?" She straightens and Biscuit run over to jump on the sofa in what he seems to think is his spot in front of the fireplace.

"My family owns a fleet of cabins. I can do just about anything that needs doing."

"That's amazing. Can I hire you?"

"I don't see why not."

"Do we need to negotiate a rate? How does that work?"

"Why don't we see how it goes? Figure it out as we go?"

She looks skeptical. "I don't know. I don't like surprises."

"I won't do anything without being upfront about what it's going to cost."

"You'll tell me first?"

"Absolutely."

Giving me a little smile that almost reaches her eyes, she takes the bag of kindling over to the hearth and sets it next to the one remaining log.

"Looks like I should have brought you firewood."

"I didn't find any around here other than what I bought at the General Store."

"Nothing against John at the General Store. He's a good friend of mine. But please don't buy firewood from him."

"Why not?"

"Because he buys it from me and upsells it to tourists."

"Oh." Her eyes widen. "Then I should buy it from you."

"Something like that."

She still hasn't figured out that I'm not going to charge her to work on anything and I'm not going to charge her for firewood.

"Want to show me what I'm going to be working on?"

"Sure. Do you want something to drink? Coffee?"

"Maybe in a minute. Before I forget, I need to show you how to work that coffee maker."

"Right. I'll be glad you did. I had instant coffee this morning."

"Tell me it isn't true."

"I'm afraid it's true."

"So that text you sent me earlier. What was that about?"

A shadow crosses her features and she cuts her eyes toward the kitchen.

"When you were here earlier, did you notice those yellow flowers? The ones in the vase?"

I follow her gaze. "No. I would have noticed them because they're my mother's favorite. Yellow daisies."

She winces. "So they weren't there? You're sure?"

"No. I'm certain of it. Why?"

"Because after you left, I went outside. I sat on the bench and talked to my sister for a few minutes. Then I came back in." She takes a deep breath. "I went to the sink for a glass of water. That's when I saw them."

"They just appeared?" A little shiver shoots down my spine.

"Yes."

"And your door was locked?"

"I'm from the city. I always lock my door. But I checked anyway."

"Do you mind if I…" I gesture toward the flowers.

"Please."

I turn the vase around, looking for anything suspicious. But they look like just ordinary flowers in an ordinary vase. Still. I don't like it.

"No idea how they got in here?"

"None. I wasn't sure what to do with them. I took a photo."

I nod. "Smart. Do you want me to take them away?"

"What are you thinking?"

"I'm thinking about taking them to the sheriff. See if he has any ideas."

"Seems a little extreme for some flowers, doesn't it?" But she bites her bottom lip nervously.

"Not when someone seemingly got them inside your house without your knowledge."

"Okay. You can take them. Maybe he can run fingerprints on them."

"Maybe." Something about them isn't sitting right with me. I'm not thinking fingerprints, but I am thinking maybe they're bugged or poisoned. "I think I'll have that coffee now after all."

"Good. Show me how."

"Where are all your mugs?" I ask, opening the cabinet where she'd found them earlier.

"I washed everything." She opens the dishwasher letting out a wisp of steam.

It seems I'm not the only one feeling a bit paranoid.

FOURTEEN

Audrey

"WANT SOME ADVICE?" Bradley asks, running a hand over one of the uneven wooden shelves in my closet.

"Of course." My hands are wrapped around the warm coffee mug. Making coffee with the fancy machine had actually been surprisingly simple. I made the coffee I'm currently holding under Bradley's watchful eye and it's as good as any designer coffee. Well. Almost.

"After we pull down all these shelves and get everything off the walls, I can add a layer of insulation then drywall on top of that."

"Drywall? You know how to do that?"

He looks at me with a raised eyebrow. "I have some experience."

"Okay." I take a sip of my coffee.

"It'll give it a clean modern appearance and with the added insulation, it'll stand the test of time."

The test of time. I take a deep breath. He guessed right that I'm planning to live here permanently. I have some plans and ideas, but all of them involve me living out my life right here in this house.

"It's big enough," he says, looking around. "You could divide it into two sections. His and hers. Once you start designing."

His and hers. I close my eyes a moment. Press my fingers against the area between my eyes. But I force myself to open them. "I don't think there's going to be a *his*."

Bradley whirls around. Sees the look on my face. "Ah Geez. I'm sorry. I wasn't thinking."

"It's okay." He's right though. It is a big closet. A REALLY big closet. And I don't have enough clothes to fill it. Brianna might. But I don't and I doubt I ever will. "I'll think about it."

"Nothing wrong with having a lot of space. And you've got plenty of time to design it." He looks away. "You said you have four other closets to do, too, right?"

"Right. You're thinking we can strip them all before we start designing."

"Makes sense. That way you have a little more time to plan out what you want to do. By the way, whoever thought to put the washer and dryer in the closer was brilliant."

"I agree completely. But." I wrinkle my nose. "They have to be replaced."

He walks over. Lifts the washer lid, makes a face as he closes it right back. "No question about that."

I bite my lip to keep from smiling. "Maybe I should have warned you."

"That would have been good of you." Just as I had done, he peeks into the dryer.

"Does anyone deliver up here?" I'm still trying not to smile.

"Not really. Not without a huge upcharge. Just go online. Order what you want from Home Depot in Boulder. I'll drive down and pick it up."

"So I'll pay you to deliver them."

"I won't charge you for that."

"Well. You should."

"I can tell you're from the city."

I look at him with one eyebrow raised, as he follows me from the closet.

"Okay," he says. "Here's what I'm thinking. You buy the supplies. I can get them for you at cost. Then you help me with the work. We'll call it even."

"I don't know anything about drywall. I can design

the closet and put in the shelves using the Elfa system, but that's about it."

"Then I'll teach you."

"Why would you do that?"

"I have a lot of reasons."

"Name one."

"I'll name two. First. It sounds like it's going to be a fun project and I like fun projects. Two. I knew Theodore Albright. He was a good man. I like to think he'd do the same for whoever moved in here if he could."

"Fair enough."

I'm not sure why, but his being so kind makes me feel weepy. I have to turn away from him and get myself in check as we head downstairs.

"It's getting late," he says. "I need to get Biscuit home. Get him something to eat."

"Right. I don't think I have any dog food." But I put it on my mental list of things to order. If Bradley and Biscuit are going to be working here, I'm going to need food for both of them.

He stops at the counter and studies the yellow daisies.

"Do you feel safe staying here by yourself?" He turns and locks his light blue eyes on mine.

I'm not sure. "Yes. I refuse to be frightened away so easily."

He grabs up the vase. "Come on Biscuit. Let's give the lady some privacy."

I swallow hard with the realization that I don't want him to leave. It's crazy but I like having him here.

"I'll go online and see about ordering the washer and dryer."

"Just let me know when it's ready. Tomorrow isn't too soon."

"Okay."

He stops at the door. "Goes without saying. Lock the doors. Don't let anyone inside."

"I know."

"Promise?"

"I promise." I bite my lip. It's like talking to one of my sisters.

"And call me if anything feels off. Or if anyone even drives up here. Anything. Anytime. Middle of the night."

"I will." I bend down to scratch Biscuit's back and let him lick my face.

"Text me about the appliances. Is tomorrow night good to start on the closets?"

"Sure. Sooner than I expected, but yeah." I stand up and reach for the doorknob. "Thank you."

"Come on Biscuit. See you tomorrow, Audrey." He strides across the front porch and starts down the stairs. "Lock the door," he says over his shoulder.

Smiling, I close the door and lock it.

I stand at the closed door and listen to the truck as he drives off.

For just a little bit of time, while Bradley was here, I hadn't felt empty inside.

It's just being in a strange place. And he's being kind.

That was all.

It has nothing to do with his mesmerizing light blue eyes and charming smile.

CHAPTER

FIFTEEN

Bradley

THE NEXT DAY, I get to the Bentley place early and go to work. Like parts of the Albright house, the closets at least, this cabin requires a lot of gutting before it can be updated.

The Bentley cabin is in a great location. Right on the river. I open up the windows and instead of turning on music, I work to the sound of the rushing river just outside.

I start in the bathroom because bathrooms are notoriously difficult. It doesn't take long for me to decide that everything has to go. I'd been thinking I could keep the toilet, but the bleach I'd left in there overnight didn't touch the rust stains.

Just as we get the toilet up, haul it out, and drop if off next to the road for trash pickup, my youngest brother Wyatt drives up in his black pickup truck that looks just like mine. We all drive them. Me. Wyatt. Caleb. Our dad. Ford F-150s in black. Workhorses. Good for pulling trailers. Hauling everything from firewood to appliances.

"Good timing," I say as he gets out of his truck.

He straightens his blue jeans jacket and takes off his sun glasses. "It's a gift."

"Wish I'd known you were coming," I say with a nod to the toilet.

"Looks like you're doing okay by yourself."

"Not really the point." I head back inside and he follows.

"I was out this way making a delivery and thought you might appreciate some help."

"Won't turn it down," I say, handing him a hammer as we step into the bathroom.

He gives the room a once over. "I see you went with my advice to gut it."

"Yeah. I was trying to avoid it."

"Something eating at you?"

I take off my baseball cap and look at my brother. "Maybe," I say. "Let's get this sink out of here."

"Heard you met the new owner of the Albright place," Wyatt says.

"Where did you hear that?" I stop what I'm doing and look up from the rusted pipes beneath the sink.

"The trees have eyes."

"Apparently." I go back to twisting the pipes loose.

"Did you turn off the water?"

"It's turned off outside."

"Is that what's eating you? I know you don't want neighbors and were hoping we could buy it."

"She doesn't bother me, but... Hand me that wrench."

"But."

I take the wrench from him. "But something odd happened up there."

"Odd as in?"

"Somebody got into her house and left a vase of flowers."

"What do you mean they got in? Why would someone do that?"

"The doors were locked. She was out back."

"Maybe the door wasn't locked."

"She claims they were and I'm inclined to believe her."

"We may have to rerun these pipes," Wyatt says.

"I figured as much. They've got some rust."

"How do you explain the flowers?"

"I can't. They're in my truck now. Gonna drop them by the sheriff's office after I leave here."

"Seems like a lot of work for some flowers."

"That's what she said. But do you remember that stalker that killed that girl over in Boulder?"

"Yeah. I remember."

"He left that girl gifts for months before he killed her."

"You think she's got a stalker?"

"I can't rule it out."

"How old is she?"

"I don't know. Our age."

"Ah."

"Ah what?" I add another pipe to our growing stack.

"Ah nothing. Just ah."

"She's my neighbor," I say. "I feel an obligation to look after her. Besides, she's fragile." Wyatt gives me a look of skepticism. "Her husband was killed in a plane crash two weeks ago."

"I read about that. Down in Texas."

"Yeah. He was flying out of Houston. I looked it up."

"That's rough."

"Yeah. Well. She somehow inherited the house. I think she's in over her head."

"How so?"

"I don't know. She's from the city."

"She'll be okay."

"You haven't seen her, Bro. She weighs about a hundred pounds and she's got these eyes that looked haunted."

"Like you said, it's fresh."

"Yeah. Well. The flowers are eating at me."

Biscuit comes running back in through the open door and deposits a squirrel at the bathroom door.

Wyatt and I look at each other.

"Where did he learn to do that?" Wyatt asks.

"Hell if I know."

"Must be a full moon."

"Maybe," I say. Whatever it is, it seems to have everything off-kilter. "You're welcome to it. Don't you eat squirrel?"

"I think he brought it to you."

Biscuit, sitting down with the squirrel in front of him, looks quite pleased with himself.

"I'll pass. Do you have time to take a cord of firewood up to the Albright place? Tomorrow would be soon enough."

"You need to tell me something?" Wyatt asks, rubbing Biscuit's head.

"No. I do not need to tell you anything. She's buying wood from the General Store and as much as I want John to stay in business, it doesn't seem right for her to pay him. Not after everything Theodore Albright did for us."

"Okay. I'll take care of it."

"Take care of that squirrel, too, would you?"

"And what are you doing?"

"I'm gonna figure out how to get this shower out of here."

Wyatt curses under his breath as he picks up the squirrel by the tail and hauls it out of here.

"Go on, Biscuit," I say. "You can at least go keep him company.

Biscuit barks once, then dutifully follows along after Wyatt.

That's when I get a text from Audrey.

"Ride down to Boulder with me?" I ask as Wyatt comes back inside.

"What's the catch?" he asks, looking at me with skepticism.

I hide a smile. "I'll buy you lunch."

CHAPTER
SIXTEEN

Audrey

THE NEXT MORNING the cleaning service shows up at my door.

The cleaning service consists of a fifty-something-year-old woman with a kind smile.

"Hi," she says when I open the door. "I'm Claire. I'm here to clean your house."

I may have promised Bradley not to open the door to anyone, but I'd been expecting someone to come by to clean the house.

"Come in," I say. I can't very well leave her standing

outside with a bucket filled with cleaning supplies sitting at her feet and a mop in one hand. "I don't think there's much to clean though."

She picks up her bucket and walks right in. "It doesn't matter. I vacuum and mop once a week whether it needs it or not."

"Really? That's why everything looks so clean."

"I've been doing it for years. You must be Audrey Sinclair. I can come back if this is a bad time."

"It's a perfect time, actually. I'm doing some cleaning myself."

"What happened?" she asks, looking a bit alarmed at the stacks of dishes, pots, pans on every surface and open cabinets to go along with them.

"I pulled everything out of the kitchen cabinets so I can clean them and wash everything."

"You're not supposed to do that," she says, rushing into the kitchen. Claire is about five two and weighs less than I do. "Let me finish this up for you."

"I'm the one who started it," I say. "Besides, I find it rather therapeutic."

She puts her hands on her hips and looks me over. "Alright then. At least let me help you. What can I do?"

"I haven't wiped down the lower cabinets yet. I've got everything out though."

She pulls her hair back with a clip and pulls on a pair of blue rubber gloves. "I'm your girl. Don't worry. I'm good at this."

"Okay then. Can I get you something to drink?"

"No, hon. I'm good. Don't you worry about me. Just pretend I'm not here. Unless you want to talk. I can do that, too."

I can tell immediately that Claire is going to be as good as she claimed to be.

"I don't like you up there on those cabinets," she says as I climb back up. "You should let me do that."

"I'm okay. I don't mind the company though."

"Okay," she says. "At least I'm here to call the ambulance."

I smile and go back to wiping down the empty cabinets. They don't really need it, but whenever I move into a new place, I feel better knowing I've wiped everything down. Just in case there are spider webs or dust or anything sticky from the previous occupants.

"I sure wish I'd known you were doing this," she says. "I would have come on up to help you."

"You're fine, Claire. After I get everything wiped down, I'm going to box up what I don't need. Is there a place in town that takes donations? Or do you know anyone who might need stuff?"

"Are you sure you don't want to keep everything? For a while at least?"

"I'm sure. I've got stuff of my own coming. And I can't stand to live in clutter."

"I hear you. I've got three daughters that live in town. Between them and their friends, I'm sure I can find someone who needs whatever you don't want to keep."

"That's great. Perfect. It might be next week before I get it all sorted and boxed up."

"I can come back anytime to help you. I'll give you my number. And you don't have to pay me. The agency pays me."

"The agency?" I dip my cleaning cloth in a bucket of cleaning water, rinse it, and squeeze it out.

"Yes. We call it the agency, but it's really just Mr. Fields. He handles everything for Mr. Albright's estate.

"Is there a lot to handle?" I wonder.

"Oh I don't know. I only met him once. I use an app to document my time. It won't let me log in unless I'm within so many feet of the house."

"That's interesting." I wonder if there are cameras. I'll have to find out how to detect for cameras and bugs and such.

"It's all high tech. But the pay's good. And I like the work."

I want to ask her about the flowers, but I don't want to let anyone else know about them just yet. Already Bradley knows and maybe the sheriff. I don't need it spreading all over town.

"Does anyone else come up here?" I ask. "to work?"

"There's a landscaping service, but they don't come inside the house."

Keys. Of course. It hadn't occurred to me until right

now that other people have keys for various things. Like Claire. Claire has a key. People would have keys to a vacant house, especially one that has people coming out regularly to keep it up.

That could easily explain how the flowers got inside.

I latch onto it as the best possible explanation.

And I make a mental note to get the locks changed.

Someone had probably brought the flowers out as a housewarming gift and since I'd been sitting out back, they hadn't known I was here.

In and out. They would have been in and out.

And I'd sent those flowers off with Bradley to take to the sheriff's office.

A classic case of overreacting.

I want to tell him right now, but I'll wait. I'll wait until he comes by later to start working on the closets.

With Claire here, this is taking half as long.

"Don't you worry," she says. "We'll have this knocked out in no time."

As much as I've enjoying my alone time, I'm happy to have Claire here to keep me company.

Having grown up with two sisters, I'm used to having someone else around. Even when I'd been married to Thomas, I'd either been at work or Thomas had been there or I'd been with one or the other of my sisters.

Besides, Claire is likeable. So far, everyone I've met in Whiskey Springs is likeable.

It's a pleasant surprise. Something I really hadn't expected when I'd packed up to drive out here.

I rinse my cloth in the water again. There was more dust in the cabinets than it looked like. It had been a good idea.

When I'd decided to move here, I really hadn't been thinking at all. I'd just reacted to the situation.

Finished with that section of the cabinets, I climb down, Claire watching me carefully, pull off my rubber gloves, and check my phone.

My washer and dryer are ready for pickup. I take a screenshot of the information and text it to Bradley.

> My order is ready for pickup, but there's no hurry. The delivery fee isn't that much, but no delivery times are available until next week. Just let me know if you'd rather I schedule the delivery.

Having to wait until next week is the thing bothering me the most. I'd found clean sheets in the linen closet and put them on the bed last night, but I'd feel a whole lot better if I could do some laundry. Even the clean sheets smell stale as was to be expected.

By the time I grab a bottle of water and twist off the cap, I have a response.

> BRADLEY
>
> Let me finish up here and I'll head that way.

"You look happy about something," Claire says.

"Oh. I ordered a new washer and dryer. Bradley is driving down to Boulder to pick them up."

Claire sits back on her heels and grins. "Bradley Winslow?"

"Yes. He's my neighbor." Of course she knows that. I don't know why I'm telling her. "He's just being kind."

"Bradley Winslow is a hottie," she says, rinsing her cloth and going back to work. "If I was thirty years younger... I'd set my cap for him."

"You're not married, Claire?" I set my phone aside and dump my dirty water out in the sink.

"Never found the right person who interested me enough for all that. I'm good just staying to myself." She sounds a little wistful.

"Things might be less complicated that way," I say, staring into space. Definitely a lot less painful.

But if I hadn't taken a risk... if I hadn't married Thomas... then I wouldn't be here right now.

I miss Thomas, there's no denying that, but I'm liking my new house.

I'm thinking tomorrow I'll go into town and explore some. Everyone seems so friendly and welcoming, I think it would be good for me.

Maybe Claire is looking for a little encouragement. "It's never too late," I tell her. "I had a great aunt who got married at eighty-years-old."

"Oh my heavens. That's too bold for me. I'm afraid I missed my chance a long time ago."

"I understand." But I really don't. Sounds to me like she had a chance once, missed it, and now she doesn't want to try again.

Even though losing Thomas was... and is... painful, I hope that one day I have the strength and the boldness to let myself love again.

CHAPTER
SEVENTEEN

Bradley

"Be nice," I tell Wyatt as I drive past my house on the way to Audrey's.

"I'm always nice," Wyatt says, looking vexed.

"Right," I say.

We'd had to wait for an afternoon storm to pass before we loaded up the washer and dryer at Home Depot.

Even though the appliances were still packed in their boxes, I put a tarp over them to make sure they stay clean and dry for the drive.

As we round the big curve, Claire passes by in her old

blue Nissan Sentra that had seen better days. Wyatt and I both hold up a hand to wave.

"Guess this was Claire's day to work," Wyatt says.

"She's a hard worker. A good woman."

"Wonder why she never got married." Wyatt wonders.

"Probably because she never set foot out of Whiskey Springs."

"I heard she was seeing Harry Pritchard for a while."

"Good God, Wyatt. Don't spread rumors like that." Harry Pritchard was a confirmed bachelor, still kicking at a hundred and one years old. In his seventies and eighties, he'd walked around town being an asshole to everyone. He'd been a banker in his younger years and I had yet to meet a person who really liked him—old or young version.

"It's not a rumor if it's true."

"Maybe. But it's definitely gossip."

I pull around to the back of Audrey's house and back up to the side door. A larger entrance and where most of the deliveries go in. It also has a covered area where firewood is stored. An area currently empty.

"You know your way around the Albright house," Wyatt comments.

"See. Gossip."

"Just stating a fact.

"Be nice."

When Audrey opens the door and steps out, Wyatt turns to me.

"Just helping out the lonely widow, huh?"

"Shut up, Wyatt."

"Hey." He unsnaps his seatbelt. "No judgement from me. Maybe she has a sister."

"She actually has two of them."

"Things are looking up."

I shoot him a look and we slide out of the truck, Biscuit along with us.

Biscuit runs up to Audrey and makes a fool of himself.

"Smart dog," Wyatt says.

"Again. Be nice."

Wyatt unsnaps the latches holding the tarp down. "I won't say another word.

"Hey," I say walking up to Audrey.

"Hey."

"We passed Claire heading out. She work out okay for you?"

"She's great. A hard worker and a nice person."

"Been coming out here most of her life from what I understand."

"Really?"

"She started working for Theodore Albright when she was a teenager."

"So they were tight?"

"I guess so."

"Huh. That might explain some things."

"Like what?"

"Nothing. Probably nothing."

"I should probably go up and disconnect the old appliances first."

"It's already done."

"How did that happen?"

"Claire and I unhooked them, slid them out, and cleaned the floor under them."

I lift my cap and scratch my head. "How did you do that?"

"Claire had a handcart in her car." She holds up a hand. "I don't understand it either, but she knew how to use it."

"Okay. Well. Come on. I'll introduce you to my brother." We walk back toward the truck where Wyatt is letting down the tailgate. "This is Wyatt."

"I'm Audrey."

"I know."

Audrey glances at me then back to Wyatt. "Thank you for helping with this."

"Not a problem," Wyatt says.

"He doesn't talk much," I tell her, shooting my brother a look. He just gives me an innocent shrug.

"That's okay."

I climb into the bed of the truck and help Wyatt unload the washer, then the dryer.

"Do we need to unbox them first?" Wyatt asks.

"Probably. Audrey, do you have an old blanket?"

"I think so." Audrey goes into the house to look for a blanket to wrap around them while we cut the boxes open.

"Try to be nice," I tell Wyatt.

"I am being nice."

I scowl at him.

"She's a widow," he says. "And you met her first. I'm just biding my time. Waiting until I can meet her sisters."

"There's something seriously wrong with you," I say, but I'm smiling to myself.

I'm rather liking this unspoken brother code Wyatt and I have going on.

I'm biding my time, too, but only because Audrey is a new widow and I have to be respectful of that.

EIGHTEEN

Audrey

I STAY out of the way while Bradley and his brother Wyatt bring my new washer and dryer into the house and somehow make hauling them upstairs look practically effortless.

I'm almost just as glad to see the old appliances go as I am to see the new ones come in. Well. Maybe not. I can't wait to start washing things.

They get everything hooked up and running without a hitch.

"What happened in the kitchen?" Bradley asks as they walk through.

"Just making room for my things."

"That's a lot of stuff," Wyatt says.

"I know. It was really packed in. Claire helped me wipe down all the cabinets. It might take me a while to sort through everything."

"I think I'd just throw it all out and start over," Wyatt says.

"Be nice," Bradley tells his brother.

"I considered doing that, but some of the stuff like the silverware is nicer than anything I own."

"Theodore Albright only bought the best."

Wyatt picks up a faded green electric can opener. "A bit dated, though."

"Do you want some help going through it?" Bradley asks.

"I think I need to go pick up my truck," Wyatt says, obviously not wanting to get caught up in the mess of sort through a bunch of stuff.

"No," I tell them both. "I'm just taking my time. Do you want to hold off on the closet?" I ask Bradley.

"I just need to run Wyatt back to his truck. I'll come back and we'll get started."

"Okay. But we really should probably wait until tomorrow. It's kinda late to start on a big project."

"She wants to wait," Wyatt tells Bradley.

"How is your day looking tomorrow?" Bradley asks.

"Good. I was thinking about going into town. Taking a look around. But no definite plans."

"How about I come by about eleven? Take you into town, show you around. We can get lunch. Then we can come back and get started on the first closet."

"Okay."

"Sounds good. Let me just find my dog and we'll get out of here."

"He's in his spot."

"He's going to ruin your couch. Come on, Biscuit."

Biscuit stands up, shakes out his hair, then leaps off the couch and races over to Bradley.

"See you in the morning then."

"Thanks again for the delivery service."

"Anytime."

I stand at the back door while they load up the old appliances into the truck then drive off around the house toward the road.

With a sigh, I go back inside, locking the door behind me.

It's getting late and I'm exhausted. I'd done more today than I had planned, but Claire was there helping so we'd worked hard. I actually did more today than I've done since Thomas's accident. I'm quite honestly exhausted.

Claire is coming back out in a couple of days to do her regular cleaning that she didn't get to do today—the vacuuming and mopping.

I go into the kitchen. Make myself a cheese and

tomato sandwich, then sit down in front of the television to eat.

With darkness settling in, the house is full of shadows. I love the large floor-to-ceiling windows with no shades in the daytime, but at night, not so much. They're just a wall of darkness. Someone could be outside looking in and I wouldn't even know it.

Fighting the chill that runs along my spine, I go around and check all the doors to make sure they're locked. I add having someone come out to install electric shades to my growing mental list of things to do.

Then just to avoid being downstairs where I can't see out, but anyone can see inside, I head upstairs and, just as I had done last night, lock my bedroom door.

While I'm at it, I'll install shades in the bedroom, too. Again, during the daytime, I love all the natural light and having the blurring of indoors with outdoors. But not so much at night.

Using the last of my firewood, I light a fire in the bedroom fireplace and climb into bed.

This is the life. A roaring fire in the bedroom. A good book to read.

Then comes the guilt.

Thomas had to die for me to be here. I feel guilty about liking it here so much.

When Brianna Facetimes me, relief washes over me.

"Hey," I say.

"Hey. Are you okay?"

"I think so. Why?"

"I just thought you would have called today."

"I got busy. The cleaning service came. Actually the cleaning service is one person. A lady named Claire. Anyway. We got all the cabinets in the kitchen wiped down."

"That sounds like a lot of work."

"It was. Oh. Hey. I want to show you something."

I slide out of bed, put on my slippers, and take my phone with me into the closet.

"Look. New washer and dryer."

"Impressive," Brianna says. I can tell she's having to force her excitement.

"I know. It's not very exciting. But I like it."

I go back and climb into bed.

"Who brought them?" she asks, obviously bored.

"Bradley went into Boulder and picked them up for me."

"Why not just have them delivered?"

"Because it would be next week before they could get here."

"That was nice of Bradley." Brianna looks a little less bored.

"It was. He has a brother named Wyatt. Wyatt doesn't have much to say."

"Strong but silent type?"

"I guess you could say that."

"Well. I'm about to head out. Having a drink with a

friend."

"Heading out? I'm already in bed."

"I know and it's an hour earlier out there."

"Well. Have fun. I'm going to read a bit, then go to sleep."

We disconnect the line.

I lay back and stare at the ceiling.

Brianna would be bored out here. There's no night life. At least not that I know of. Or even care to know about.

Lilah. She might be okay because she can paint. She's like me in that way. We're introverts unlike our sister. Brianna needs a lot of stimulation to keep her happy.

I don't think she'd find that in Whiskey Springs.

I feel a little sad knowing that my dream of having my sisters come out here to live with me in this big old house is only going to remain a dream.

And I don't know. I might not always like it here. But for now it suits me.

Picking up the novel I'm reading, a fairy smut book that had me turning pages when I started it two weeks ago, but lately I've had trouble concentrating on, I get through about two paragraphs before I find my mind wandering to a ruggedly handsome man with light blue eyes who wants to help me with my closet project and take me to lunch tomorrow.

I close my eyes and try to force my thoughts somewhere else. Not on Thomas. That way lies sadness.

A wolf howls somewhere in the distance, its mournful cry echoing the way I feel right now.

Something is most definitely wrong with me.

I try not to think about Thomas too much and it seems wrong to think about Bradley.

Picking up my book, I force my thoughts to travel to and stay in a fictional world with a heartbreakingly handsome fairy whose love for a mortal woman knows no bounds.

CHAPTER
NINETEEN

Bradley

Before I head up to Audrey's to pick her up for lunch, I make a run down the hill into town.

It might be full on summer for a whole lot of the rest of the country, but here perched high in the Colorado mountains, it's still springtime. The river rushes with snowmelt. Trees stretch with tender new leaves. Baby elk dart through the underbrush like secrets not meant to be seen. Everything feels on the verge of something. The season. Me.

I drive past a bulldozer working on repairing a section of road damaged over the winter. Fortunately it wasn't bad enough to shut down the road, but the town is good about keeping repairs up on the roads so they don't become impassable.

I slide into a parking spot in front of the sheriff's office and take the yellow daisies inside with me.

"Bradley," Maggie, the receptionist says batting her eyes teasingly. "you know you shouldn't have."

"Actually I should have, but unfortunately, these are possible evidence."

No point in trying to hide anything from Maggie. Like Wyatt says, the trees have eyes... and ears.

"Evidence? What is the world coming to? Wait. You're serious? Has someone been hurt?"

"Not yet. And I hope it's nothing. I REALLY hope it's nothing. But I want to see what Sheriff Morgan thinks."

"Go on back, Dear. He's working at his desk."

"Got a minute?" I stop at Sheriff Morgan's door and give him time to look up.

He removes his reading glasses and smiles at me. "Come in Bradley. Have a seat."

Sheriff Morgan is only about ten years old than I am, but he looks a lot older. Gray hair. Wrinkles around his eyes. A perpetual frown that he constantly fights. Comes with the territory of being sheriff and even though Whiskey Springs is a peaceful town, he works hard to keep it that way.

He's actually been looking a lot better since he got married a couple of years ago.

"I hope those yellow daisies aren't going to cause me to lose any sleep."

"Yeah. I'm with you on that. I'm just being proactive and overly cautious." I set the vase of flowers on his desk.

Then I tell him what happened with the flowers.

"Did you know that Audrey was moving in?" I ask him.

"I knew it." A tall man in good shape, but by no means small, he leans back in his chair and laces his fingers behind his head. "A lot of people have keys to the Albright place."

"I didn't really consider that."

"It's not something we'd normally give much thought to around here."

"Do you think it's anything to worry about? I keep thinking about that girl in Boulder. The one who was stalked by that guy."

"Yeah. I know the one." He sits up. Looks at me with big brown eyes that I'd hate to be on the wrong side of. "I won't discount it and say it's nothing. I'd honestly be surprised if it turns out to be anything. But having said that, I'm going to hold onto these. We can always run prints. If something happens and we need to."

Something about the order of that way of thinking seems off to me. Maybe because I've met Audrey and I like her. "Seems like we should run prints now rather than after something happens."

"I'm not seeing just cause. Let me think on it. Do some

asking around. See if there's been any other similar activity around."

"Okay," I say, biting back anything else I might want to say. I hadn't expected to feel worse leaving out of the sheriff's office than I had when I'd come in. But I do. "Thanks for taking your time to see me."

"Bradley," Sheriff Morgan says, stopping me at the door. I turn. "Keep your eyes open. I don't mean to put any extra responsibility on you, but you live closest to the Albright place. To Audrey."

"Right."

"If you see anything out of order, call me."

"Don't worry. I'll take care of it." With a nod, I head out the door. "See you later Maggie."

By the time I'm back in my truck, I've decided that I'd wasted my time going to see Sheriff Morgan.

I'd planned on watching out for her anyway. I don't need someone telling me to do that.

CHAPTER
TWENTY

Audrey

WITHOUT A CLOSET TO stand and stare into, I kneel on the floor in front of my three open suitcases and try to figure out what to wear.

What does a person wear to lunch in Whiskey Springs?

Not a dress or a skirt. I rule that out fairly quickly.

Boots. Hiking boots would be preferable. But since I don't have any hiking boots—another thing for the shopping list—I go with my lace-up ankle boots. They're comfortable enough and it's not like we're going to be walking into town. We're going to be driving. Not hiking.

So now that I have my footwear picked out, I decide on a pair on blue jeans. Then I consider a sweatshirt, but no, a sweatshirt is too sloppy for my first day in town.

Being seen with Bradley Winslow, I'll probably meet some people. And even if I don't meet people, people will see me and they'll talk. I don't want to be that sloppy widow who's living in the Albright house.

I narrow it down to a white button-down shirt like I would have worn to work or a sweater.

I lay my options out on the bed and get into the shower.

By the time I get dressed, I've decided on the button-down shirt. It's a classic and dresses up the jeans.

Dressed, I take my time drying out my hair, then use a hot brush to smooth it out even more.

I want to make a good impression and it has absolutely nothing to do with it being sort of like a date with Bradley.

Not a date. I've hired him to help me with my closets.

But...since he's not charging me for the work, though, that could possibly change things.

Still, I tell myself as I blend in some foundation and a swipe on little bit of eyeshadow.

It's not a date. It's just lunch. He's being kind to take his time to show me around town. He knows I'm new here and he's trying to make me feel welcome.

When the doorbell rings at ten fifteen, I nearly jump out of my skin.

Bradley isn't supposed to be here until eleven. Fortunately, I'd gone ahead and gotten ready early.

I smear on some lip gloss, then head downstairs.

I don't see Bradley's truck when I look out the window. Instead, I see the tail lights of a jeep driving off.

That's odd.

I watch out the window for several minutes, waiting to see if anything looks out of the ordinary.

Maybe the jeep had been lost. But someone had rang my doorbell.

I need to move changing the locks up on the priority list.

The locks for the doors and the shades for the windows. In fact, those both need to move ahead of the closets. I'll ask Bradley if he can recommend someone for either or both of those. I'd rather get a recommendation than just using google.

Not being from here, I'm not sure I trust someone I find on the Internet. Not without a recommendation.

I head back into the kitchen and use the thirty minutes or so I have before Bradley gets here to sort through some of the things I pulled out of the kitchen cabinets. It's turned into a full-time job.

When I hear Bradley's truck coming toward the house, I breathe a sigh of relief.

I've really got to stop being so jumpy.

It's going to be hard to live here when I'm so jumpy all the time.

After watching Bradley step out of his truck, I open the door.

"Where's Biscuit?" I ask.

"He's staying with Wyatt today. Taking him into a restaurant in town is frowned upon."

"Oh." I'd been looking forward to see the dog and hadn't even realized it.

"We can stop and pick him up after lunch."

"Okay."

"Were you expecting some packages?" he asks.

"I don't know. Maybe. Why?"

"Cause the mailman left you a stack of boxes."

I look to my right and sure enough, there's a stack of half a dozen boxes there. My handwriting. My boxes. Things I'd had Brianna put in the mail.

"They got here fast."

"Your stuff from Houston?"

"Yeah." I put a hand on the door frame to steady myself. "Someone rang the doorbell and... I've really got to work on not being so jumpy."

"I think it's natural living out here by yourself. In a strange place."

"I didn't know it was the mailman. I thought... I didn't know what to think."

"The mailman drives an old jeep," he says.

"So I gather."

"Can I bring these inside for you?"

"Please. That would be great."

After he hauls the boxes inside, he stands just inside the door and looks at me.

"Audrey," he says.

"Yes?" I swallow hard.

"I know it's not good to be jumpy all the time, but whatever you do..." He sweeps a strand of hair back off my face. "Don't stop being cautious. Okay?"

"Okay. I won't."

Right now he could have asked me just about anything and I probably would have agreed. My heart is pounding. My blood pumping through my veins.

"You ready to get some lunch?"

"Ready."

I hope he doesn't notice my hands are shaking just a little as I grab my purse and meet him back at the door.

It might not be a date, but it's my first outing into town.

As he opens the passenger door of his truck and waits while I climb inside, I admit to myself that it's close enough to a date to count in my book.

Maybe being a widow changes one's perspective. Or maybe it's just being out here by myself living in this big old house, but whatever it is, I have to remind myself to be careful.

I could get in over my head really quick with Bradley. Too quick.

TWENTY-ONE

Bradley

"THAT'S my little cabin through the trees there." I point out as we pass by my place.

Squinting she leans forward.

"It's hard to see, I know."

"It's cute. Cozy," she says. "The kind of place I probably would have chosen for myself."

"You don't like the big house?" I ask, glancing over, but keeping my eyes on the road. The drive along the mountainside is precariously narrow in places. It's clear now, but when I'd headed into town earlier, there had been a layer of fog below the road. Not above, but below. Simply a testament to how high up in elevation we are.

"I like it." She takes a deep breath. "I have mixed feelings about it, I guess."

"Like what?"

"Like if I had my sisters here, I think it would be great. But with just me, it's a little unsettling. I don't think it's the size of the house though. I'm thinking I need to change the locks and see about installing some electric shades for the windows. Just for at night."

"You got spooked right off the bat with those flowers."

"Yeah." She takes a deep breath, lets it out slowly. "What did the sheriff say?"

I don't want to tell her he blew it off as nothing. Not when that might cause her to let her guard down.

"Typical. He's going to check around. See if there have been any other incidents."

"So nothing." She looks out the window. "It's probably nothing anyway. I'm sure a lot of people have keys. Maybe somebody was dropping off a housewarming gift and didn't know I was home."

A person dropping off a housewarming gift should let themselves be known. Not leave flowers with no name. "I know a guy who can change out the locks. I'll give you his phone number."

"Thank you."

"Sure. Happy to do it."

"I don't remember the road being so narrow."

"You had to come this way on your way in."

"It was late and I was too tired to pay much attention," she says with a tight little smile.

We turn right onto the main highway leading into town.

I want to take the veil of sadness off her. I know it's not possible. It's something only time can do. All I can do is hope to distract her just a little bit.

"Is a hamburger okay?" I ask. "The Hungry Biscuit has the best burgers and fries around."

"A hamburger sounds good."

"The Hungry Biscuit it is."

I pull into the crowded parking lot and find an open space around back.

"It's busy," she says.

"Known for the best burgers and fries in the state."

"In the state. That's a bold claim."

"I'm curious to see if you agree. I'll come around. Get the door."

"I'm curious, too."

I slide out of the truck and walk around to open her door.

I haven't dated anyone since Zoe. That was three years ago. She'd had her sights set on California from the beginning. I'd hoped she would change her mind, but she'd gotten out of here so fast it made a man's head spin.

I was now considered the most eligible and most

confirmed bachelor of Whiskey Springs. It wasn't a distinction I'd asked for, but I couldn't deny the truth of it either.

With my family owning Timber Ridge Cabins and me being the oldest male in the family, there was nothing I could say to dispute it. It didn't even seem to matter that our company was going to be split equally into three parts after we inherited it.

Maybe being seen with Audrey would get the scheming women off my heels.

After I open the passenger door and Audrey slides to the ground, her feet wobble on the uneven rocky surface.

I steady her with a hand on her arm.

"It's a little difficult to walk on this," I say.

"I noticed."

I slide my hand down her arm and press my palm against hers, linking our fingers, as we step away from the truck. She doesn't pull away.

Together, we walk around toward the front door of The Hungry Biscuit.

A cheerful bell rings above the door as we step inside. The scent of grilled onions and fresh-baked bread—comfort food and memories—fills my senses. A couple of locals glance up from their booths, then go back to their burgers.

She pauses just inside the door and takes a look around.

"I love this place already," she says, her voice light. "Quirky name. Smells amazing. And... I've never been welcomed to lunch by a giant hamburger before."

She's referring to the human-sized cardboard hamburger just inside the door, cheerful and absurd in the best small-town way.

I grin. "They're proud of their burgers."

A waitress waves us to a corner booth, the kind with worn red vinyl and a window view of the mountains. Audrey slides in across from me, tucking her hair behind her ear.

"So," I say, picking up a menu. Handing it to her. Then taking one for myself. "You more of a cheeseburger-and-fries girl or... grilled chicken salad with dressing on the side?"

She raises an eyebrow. "That seems like a rather odd question."

I lean in, lowering my voice just enough to make her smile. "It means I'm trying to learn your deepest secrets. Starting with your burger order."

She laughs—a real, honest laugh that warms something in my chest and gives me hope.

"Well," she says, studying the menu with a mock-serious expression, "you'll be pleased to know I'm a cheeseburger and fries, extra pickles and tomato, kind of girl."

"Dangerous," I say, smiling. "I like it."

And for the first time in a long while, something feels easy. Like maybe this isn't just lunch. Like maybe it could be something more. Something more than I had even with Zoe. Even with Zoe, things had never felt quite right.

Audrey is different.

And so far she's not talking about going anywhere.

TWENTY-TWO

Audrey

RETRO MUSIC with nostalgia drifts from hidden speakers. Eighties tunes, maybe, from what I can hear.

The Hungry Biscuit has gone all in on branding. Their logo—a cartoon hamburger with a wide grin and tiny arms—adorns everything in sight. It's stamped on the napkins, printed on the paper placemats, even printed on the back of the laminated menus.

On the walls, framed photos of customers through the decades hang beside retro ads proclaiming Hot 'n Flaky Since '62! There's a black-and-white mural of a hamburger wearing sunglasses and snow skiing down a mountainside. A string of mismatched café lights zigzags overhead, casting a soft glow on red vinyl booths and chrome-edged tables that look like they've been here since the last century.

Near the register, a display case houses hamburger-themed merchandise—mugs, bumper stickers, even T-shirts that read The Hungry Biscuit — Whiskey Springs Original Hamburgers.

"I'm getting the idea that the Hungry Biscuit started here in Whiskey Springs."

"It did. It's in all the small towns now. Alpine Falls. Silver Pines."

"Cute."

He looks comfortable sitting on the other side of the booth.

One arm relaxed across the back of his seat.

"So The Hungry Biscuit." I lean forward and look into Bradley's light blue eyes. "Is it hamburgers or biscuits?"

"Hamburgers."

"Then why biscuit?"

"Biscuit is a generic term like widget."

"Is that why you named your dog Biscuit?"

He grins. "Something like that."

I nod, trying to keep a straight face. "It must be a Colorado thing."

"You don't have biscuits in Texas?"

"We have biscuits. But a hamburger is a hamburger and a biscuit is a biscuit."

"Fair enough. Tell me something you say that we don't."

"That's easy. We say y'all."

"That's a universal southern thing."

A waitress stops at our table. "Hey Bradley." She looks at me. "Hi."

"Hi."

"Evie, this is Audrey."

"Hi Audrey." She puts a hand on her hip. "What can I get for the two of you?"

Bradley looks at me.

"I'll just have a coke."

"Same for me," Bradley says.

"Be right back," Evie says.

"That's one," Bradley says.

"What's one?"

"Coke. I would have asked for a soda."

"Right." I lean forward. "Do you know everyone in town?"

"I guess I do. Unless they're tourists or just passing through."

"Are there any tourists here now?"

"There are. See that family over there? The one with the two parents, a little boy and a little girl? Tourists."

I look over my shoulder. "Anyone else?"

"I don't think so."

"Do you all like tourists?"

"Tourists are our bread and butter. We wouldn't have much of a town without them, certainly not Timber Cabins."

"Makes sense. What about new people? People who aren't from around here?"

"We welcome new people with open arms. Not everyone is lucky enough to be born and raised here."

"That's promising."

"What about your life back in Houston? You don't think you'll miss it?"

"Sometimes, but…" I look over at the whimsical hamburger painted on the wall. "There were a lot of things that I didn't like."

"Such as?"

"I didn't like living in the suburbs. And I didn't care for my job either. I just couldn't find a way out of it."

"You worked at an art gallery, right?"

"Right."

The server drops off our cokes and I take a sip of the sparkling, bubbling soda.

"But you didn't like it?"

I shake my head. "I didn't dislike it. It just didn't feel like what I wanted to do with my life. You know?"

"I do know. What is it you want to do?"

"I haven't figured that out yet. You'd think that by the

time someone is twenty-seven, they'd have figured out what they want to do when they grow up."

"Maybe." He shrugs. "Maybe you just needed to change perspective to find it."

"That's what I'm hoping."

"You'll figure it out," he says. "When it comes to you, you'll know."

CHAPTER
TWENTY-THREE

Bradley

AFTER LUNCH, we walk down to the General Store.

"You should be able to get some of the things on your list here," he says.

"Maybe," she looks around at the rows and rows of everything from cans of paint to paintings for the wall.

"Do they have new door locks?"

"I think they do."

I lead her toward hardware to a section of door locks.

"He can order something else if you want something different."

"I've been looking online. I'm thinking something with a keypad and a camera."

"John won't have that, but he can get it for you."

"I can just order something online." She turns and looks at me with her meadow green eyes. "Do you think you could install new locks?"

"I don't see why not."

"When we get back, I'll show you what I'm thinking. You can tell me if it'll work on my door."

"I can make it work. But I'll look at it. Make sure it's compatible."

"Okay. I need shades for my windows."

"We'll definitely have to special order those. I'll help you measure and I can install those, too."

"Seriously?"

"Sure. It's not that hard."

"You're rather handy to have around."

"So I've been told."

"Really? Who else told you that?"

"Mostly little old ladies with blue hair."

She laughs out loud.

She needed to get out. To think about something other than what happened to Thomas.

"Okay. So we're making progress. What else do you need?"

"Hiking boots," she says.

"Hiking boots? I didn't expect you to say that."

"They aren't for the house."

"Funny girl, aren't you?"

She shrugs. "I've been told."

"Definitely funny. So we need to go across the street for hiking boots. Anything else in here?"

"I could use a black marker and some trash bags."

"John definitely has those."

A few minutes later, a paper sack in my hand with a marker and a roll of trash bags, we head across the street to the ladies' clothing shop.

"Are you sure they have hiking boots?" she asks as we step inside. "It looks more like a place to get something formal to wear."

"Hello Bradley," a young lady greets Bradley from behind the counter. "How can I help you?" She shifts her gaze over to me.

"We need some hiking boots," I say.

"Of course. Back left corner. Let me know if you need help."

"I will. Thanks Steph."

The back of the shop is literally a wall of shelves with two benches in front for sitting. Stacks of shoe boxes. Boots. High heels. Sneakers.

Audrey wanders to the hiking boot section.

"See anything you like?"

She picks up a basic lace-up hiking boot in black leather. "These look good."

"Try them on. What size do you wear?"

"A six."

I stretch up over her head and pull down a box.

She sits on one of the benches and slips off her own lace-up boots. City boots. I open up the box and pick up one of the boots. The laces are still wrapped up in tissue. I get the laces started, then hand the boot over.

She slides it on her foot and starts lacing it up.

"Ouch." She jerks her hand back. "I think I broke a fingernail."

"Not surprising with all the housework you've been doing. You really need to let Claire do that."

"I have to have something to do." She lightly touches her broken fingernail.

"I know. Let me do this." I slide onto the floor, kneeling in front of her, and get to work on lacing up her boots.

"Handy," she says, looking down at me.

"I know. I'm a sucker for a pretty girl."

Out of the corner of my eye, I watch the elusive smile tug at her lips.

I'm betting she's smiled more in the last two hours than she smiled in the last two weeks.

She sits quietly while I lace up one boot, then slide the other one on and lace it up, too.

"How do they feel?" I ask, after I have both of them securely laced up and tied. I hold out a hand to help her stand up.

"They feel good," she says.

"You might have to break them in," I say.

"Hiking maybe?"

"That can be arranged."

"You'd go hiking with me?"

"I can't very well let you go by yourself." She raises a brow. "Bears and mountain lions."

"Somehow that doesn't make me feel very safe."

"I never walk anywhere without my can of bear spray."

"And I feel safe again."

She grins at me and my heart melts.

She's a widow. She's a widow. She's a widow.

She's not available for me to be thinking about romantically.

I need to keep my head about me. And yet it's virtually impossible with her looking at me with her siren green eyes.

TWENTY-FOUR

Audrey

Wearing my new hiking boots, I walk with Bradley, carrying a shopping bag with my old boots, down Main Street.

Whiskey Springs is a quintessential small town with three traffic lights. Two way traffic with parallel parking on either side of the street. Half a dozen or so people driving up and down the street. About twice that many more walking the sidewalks.

An older couple holds hands as they cross the street. The family we'd seen earlier at the Hungry Biscuit step into the ice cream parlor. Two teenage boys with backpacks punch each other playfully as they walk home from school.

Tall, snow-capped mountains rise behind the town, cradling it like protective giants frozen in time. Their jagged peaks pierce the sky, a stark contrast to the quiet charm nestled in the valley below where time slows and every breath carries the scent of pine and possibility.

The faint aroma of firewood smoke lingers in the crisp air and swirls with the rich scent of cappuccinos from the corner coffee shop. As we pass the ice cream parlor, the sugary sweetness wraps around us, warm and nostalgic despite the chill.

New spring growth stretching out on the spruce trees. Tender spring flowers flutter in the soft breeze. Blue butterfly begonias. Salmon-colored geraniums. Pink and white petunias.

My new home.

We leave the main sidewalk and walk along a path leading to the bubbling river. A wooden plank bridge arches over the river leading to a little sitting area on the other side.

Wooden benches. A community of painted bird houses.

"It's beautiful here," I say, sitting on one of the benches.

"It's beautiful all year around," Bradley says. "And at Christmas everything is lit up with twinkling, festive lights. There's nothing else like it."

"I'm looking forward to seeing it," I say. "I'm especially looking forward to winter. To the snow."

"Yeah. The first snowfall is magical."

"And after that?"

He stretches out his long legs. Crosses them at the ankles. "After that depends on a lot of factors. I don't want to say too much that would influence your decision."

"Sounds a bit ominous."

"It's beautiful. You're going to love it."

"You're not all that convincing. Will we get snowed in?"

"One of those factors. Each year is a little bit different from the last. But the short answer is not usually." He takes a breath. "Unless there's a blizzard."

"I hope you're not on one of the tourist committees."

He laughs. "I'm on the town council."

I look over at him. Nod slowly. His ruggedly good looks would easily compensate for anything negative he might say about Whiskey Springs. Not that he's being negative. He's just being realistic. And it's probably because I live here now. As such, I should know the real scoop.

"You don't want me to have any unrealistic expectations?"

"I wouldn't want that."

"And since I'm not a tourist, you can tell me the truth."

"I try to always tell the truth."

"That's a good quality to have." Closing my eyes, I take a deep breath, inhaling the scent of blue spruce trees all around us. Let it out slowly. The melodic trickling of the river soothes me.

"Have you spent much time in the mountains?" he asks.

"This is my first time."

"So you just got in your car and headed up here with no idea of what to expect? No idea about whether you would like it here?"

"Pretty much." I open my eyes and meet his gaze.

"I would think that would take a lot of bravery." His eyes are kind. Understanding. And questioning.

"I'm not sure I would call it bravery," I say. "Maybe more like a sort of desperation. I didn't know what else to do."

"That didn't involve moving in with relatives."

"Right." I'd told him about that. "I told you about my husband and the plane crash."

He nods. "I'm sorry," he says softly.

I nod. "I wish that were the whole story."

He waits. Doesn't push. Just watches me like he's actually listening.

"I found out afterward, from his attorney, that he had a child. With someone else. A child I didn't know existed."

His brow furrows, but he says nothing.

"He left everything—everything—to the child's

mother. Except this house." I struggle to keep my tone even. To keep the bitterness and hurt out of my tone. I take a deep breath. Let it out slowly. "And a monthly stipend arranged through some kind of legal arrangement set up by Theodore Albright."

"You must be furious."

"I don't know what I am. Angry, yes. Betrayed. Grieving. But it's not... clean. It's not like I can just hate him and move on."

I glance away, blinking fast. "I didn't come here to fall apart. I came here because I already had."

The words hang between us.

I draw a deep ragged breath. "It sounds pathetic."

"It doesn't," he says gently. "It sounds like you're surviving something most people wouldn't know how to face."

I look away again, blinking back fresh tears. His kindness cuts deeper than I expect—like it's peeling away a layer I didn't realize was there.

Thinking back, I realize... Thomas wasn't a very good listener. Not really. He and I had something, yes. But right now, I'm not sure what that something even was.

Everything feels like it was built on a foundation of half-truths and silence.

I'd done the math. The child came before me—before we even met. And somehow, that makes the betrayal worse. Because it wasn't just about what he did. It was about what he hid. He married me without ever telling me. Lived every day beside me with that secret buried like a landmine between us.

I go quiet, the words catching in my throat now, too heavy to carry any further.

He doesn't try to fill the silence. He just sits there, close but not crowding me, his presence steady. Solid. Like he's offering something I didn't even know I needed.

After a moment, I exhale slowly and lean my head against his shoulder. He doesn't flinch or shift or say a single thing.

He just lets me rest there.

And for the first time in what feels like forever, I don't feel like I'm drowning.

A few seconds pass. Then his arm slips around me—slowly, carefully—like he's making sure it's okay, even without asking.

I don't pull away. I don't want to.

I let myself lean into him just a little more. Not because I'm ready for anything. Just because right now... it feels safe.

And safe is more than I expected to find.

TWENTY-FIVE

Bradley

"You're good help," I say, handing Audrey a chunk of wood I pulled from the closet with a crowbar.

She's wearing a pair of my work gloves that are too two sizes too big for her and an oversized sweatshirt that she changed into after we got back here to her house.

"You seem surprised," she says, coming back from adding the chunk of wood to a big cardboard box we'd designated as debris.

"Well, you are a city girl," I say teasingly. After our moment near the river, I'm purposely trying to keep the mood light.

"Never underestimate a girl from the city," she says. "You never know what we'll be able to do."

"I stand corrected. How are the washer and dryer working out?"

"Great. Couldn't be happier."

Her phone chimes. "It's my sister. If I don't answer, she'll send out the National Guard."

"Go ahead. I need to take Biscuit out for a walk anyway."

"Okay." She walks off, answering her phone.

I take a look around. Most of the demolition work is done on this closet. Just one more closet to go and tomorrow I can start floating the sheetrock.

I find that Biscuit followed Audrey downstairs and is already out back with her making his rounds, so I make a detour by the refrigerator for a bottle of water.

Audrey has got quite the mess in here. Unopened boxes of her own things that she had sent up stacked along one wall.

A row of half-filled boxes of things labeled *donate, discard*, and *keep (maybe)*.

Then there are the things she's still going through.

Maybe later, after we finish peeling the old out of the closets, she'll let me help her go through what looks like a lot of junk left here by Theodore.

People live somewhere long enough, they pack things in.

I understand Audrey wanting to start with a clean

slate. I did the same thing when I moved into my cabin. Except that it was on a much smaller scale and it wasn't packed with someone else's stuff.

But take the Bentley cabin. Gutting the bathroom to start from the ground up. It's a lot of work, but it'll be worth it when it's finished.

The cabin has good bones. Most of them built back in the last century do. They just need to be modernized up to this century. Then they're good to go.

While I drink my water, I watch Audrey pacing along her back deck. I haven't met her sisters, but it seems like they might be a bit overprotective. It's understandable after what she went through. And then the way she'd loaded up and come up here. By herself.

She said she didn't have a choice, but there's always a choice. She chose to come up here by herself over moving back in with her parents or moving in with her sisters.

She hadn't said anything about getting her own place, but I can only imagine that had something to do with her finances.

From what she told me, her husband left her in something of a bind. Apparently her work at the art gallery didn't pay enough for her to get her own place.

Biscuit paces along beside her, matching her step by step. She idly pets the top of his head as she walks.

She's a good person, Audrey Sinclair. I'm going to do what I can for her.

And hopefully give her the space to heal.

In the meantime, I have to remind myself not to push her into something she might regret later. I don't want her feeling guilty because of me.

TWENTY-SIX

Audrey

"My goodness gracious," Claire says when she steps into the kitchen. "How on earth did you get everything sorted and put up? When I left here two days ago, I didn't think you were ever going to dig your way out of all this stuff we pulled out of the cabinets."

"I had a little help," I say. A lot of help if I was being honest.

Bradley had been amazing. He had an amazing attitude about not keeping things that I knew I didn't need.

And then to make things even better, he'd loaded up

the boxes of donations in his truck and gotten it all out of here along with my empty boxes.

"It looks amazing," Claire says, running a hand along the uncluttered countertop.

"Everything's organized," I say, opening one of the overhead cabinets.

"You've got four plates on one shelf. Four glasses on another and nothing on the top shelf."

"I know. It's great. My mugs are over here." I open another cabinet to show her my three coffee mugs.

"I've never seen a kitchen so organized. Maybe in a magazine."

"It's so big. I have a place for everything."

"And everything in its place. Well," she says. "I came prepared to work. But it looks like I'll just be doing my normal vacuuming and cleaning."

"You're making me feel bad," I say.

"Don't feel bad. I really am impressed."

"I couldn't have done it without Bradley."

Claire's face lights up. "You could do a lot worse than Bradley Winslow."

"He's just being helpful."

"I know. I know. But that's as good a place to start as any."

I can't help the little smile that plays about my lips. "Don't you go starting any rumors," I say. "He's very kind."

Claire doesn't know the real reason why I'm here. She

doesn't know that everything my husband and I had saved went toward his bills. That his life insurance went to a child he had with another woman. People I didn't even know about until the attorney told me after the accident.

That I'd come here because I needed a place to heal.

That I came here because I was broken.

Not to get into a relationship, no matter how kind... and hot... Bradley Winslow might be.

"He's never been married," she says.

I cut my eyes at her.

She holds up a hand. "I'm just 'saying. But I'm getting to work now. I've got a house to clean."

While Claire goes upstairs and vacuums, I got out back and bring in an armful of firewood from the stack Wyatt had dropped off yesterday. He'd brought a trailer full of chopped firewood and stacked it in a covered area behind the house. A cord, they'd called it. I called it a ton of firewood.

I lay the logs in the fireplace, add some kindling, and strike a match.

Within minutes, I have a healthy fire going. Everyone else would say it was too big, but I rather like a big fire.

Settling myself on the sofa, I open up a box, about the size of a shoe box, and face a task I've been putting off.

It's time to send thank you notes to people who sent flowers and brought food to my house after Thomas's accident. Mostly people who worked with Thomas. The people at Skye Travels were all so very kind. Even his boss, Noah Worthington and his wife Savannah had stopped by my house. They'd brought a lush green potted ivy and a homemade apple pie.

They'd asked if there was anything they could do. I honestly think they'd meant it. And they hadn't stayed more than a few minutes. I appreciated that.

Other than the Worthingtons, the names are a blur. I don't recognize any of the others. But they were there. And I have to thank them for being supportive.

CHAPTER

TWENTY-SEVEN

Bradley

I'M right in the middle of floating the sheetrock at the Bentley cabin when I get a call from the Sheriff.

With the windows open, the sounds of the river drift in a cool breeze. It's one of those cool, cloudy days that make me feel sorry for people who live in places like Nevada and Texas.

Only in the Colorado mountains can we be full on summer and have a pleasant day with highs in the fifties.

There is nowhere else I'd rather live.

"Hello, Sheriff," I say, walking out of the cabin's bathroom that is currently undergoing a complete trans-formation.

"Hello Bradley. I just wanted to give you a quick update. I made some calls. There haven't been any reports of missing girls or even any cases of stalking in the neighboring counties, at least nothing out of the ordinary."

"So no active serial killers."

"I don't think Audrey has anything to worry about. Just someone with a key who did something they shouldn't have."

"Right." Like go inside her house and leave a vase a yellow daisies. Flowers with no name. No indication of who they came from.

Not a very nice thing to do.

"So rest your mind," he says. "I recommend she change the locks for her own peace of mind."

"Got new locks on order."

"Good. Good. Just wanted to tell you what I knew."

"Thanks for the update." I disconnect the line.

I'm still feeling unsettled about it all. No matter what the sheriff says, I still don't trust that Audrey is safe. I'm just being overprotective. That has to be it.

When I finish up here, I'll go by her place. See if those door locks came in yet. Maybe stop in town and pick up a pizza. If the door locks aren't in yet, we can start measuring for the blinds. There's plenty to do over at Audrey's place. Enough to keep us busy for days.

And one thing I'd learned last night is that she needs help.

I know it's the grief, but sometimes she'll just stop what she's doing and stare into space. It's as though her mind freezes and she can't make decisions.

I'd convinced her, and rightly so, that she doesn't need all that stuff Theodore left behind. A lot of it was from the last century. She kept some of his really high quality silverware and some china, but things like the old green can opener had to go.

Audrey had brought some nice things with her. Between what she kept of his and what she brought of hers, she has a nice setup in the kitchen.

The sooner I can get her closet rounded out, the sooner she can move her clothes into her closet and start feeling like she's got a permanent home there.

I'm being selfish about that. I want to make sure she feels like she belongs. I want her to belong. To stay.

By mid-afternoon, I'm ready to knock off here and head to Audrey's place. If Wyatt isn't busy, I'll ask him to come by tomorrow. Help me make some progress on the Bentley place. We're nearing peak tourist season and the longer I drag my feet on it, the longer it'll be before we can rent it out to someone and start recouping the money spent to buy and renovate it.

As much as I enjoy what I do, I have to keep in mind that we have a business.

I pack up my tools, haul them to the truck and, with

Biscuit in tow, climb up into the cab of the truck and head toward Audrey's place.

Too early to get a pizza. I can drive back in later and get something. Even better, take Audrey with me. It'll be good for her to get out of the house.

I pass by my own cabin without so much as a twinge.

Just as I'm pulling up to Audrey's, Claire is pulling out.

She waves at me and I can already hear the rumors getting started.

I don't care if people talk. I don't care what they say about me spending time over here. Really, Claire is the only one who's seen me here. But people have seen us in town together now.

That's more than enough to give the gossips plenty to talk about.

Audrey doesn't meet me at the door like she usually does.

When she does open the door a couple of minutes later, her eyes are red-rimmed like she's been crying.

TWENTY-EIGHT

Audrey

"ARE YOU OKAY?" Bradley asks as I open the door.

"Yes," I say, pushing my hair back. "I hadn't realized it was so late."

"It's not late. I'm early."

"Hey Biscuit." I lean over and hug the dog, taking a moment of comfort in him, then step back giving them room to come inside. "Claire just left."

"I know. I passed her on the road. It smells good in here. Like vanilla and some kind of flowers. Daffodils maybe."

"Claire did that. I don't know what she did, but everything feels so clean."

"It's nice to get the house cleaned up. What's all that?" he asks with a nod toward the papers spread over the coffee table in front of the roaring fire in the fireplace. Writing these letters makes me sad. In an odd way, writing the thank you notes seems to finalize the end of my life with Thomas.

"Just some letters I have to write."

I go over and gather them up, putting them back in their Kraft-colored box.

"Don't put them away on my account."

"It's okay. I don't want to look at them anymore tonight."

I don't have to tell him they have something to do with Thomas. He knows. I know he knows.

"Anything I can help with?" he asks.

"Nothing you want to get involved in. Just letters I should have written already."

"I'm sure people understand."

I give him a sideways look. Then change the subject. "The doorknobs haven't come in yet."

"It's okay. We can finish up that last closet if you want to."

"Okay and then I guess we can start measuring for window shades."

"That's what I was thinking." He turns and looks toward the tall windows at the side of the house. Out at the magnificent view of the mountains. "It seems a waste to block those views."

"It's just for night time. And just until things settle down."

"Right."

I know better. I know that things will never settle down enough for me to feel safe enough to have bare windows at night.

"You look tired," he says. "We don't have to do any work at all if you don't want to."

I nod slowly. "What do you want to do?"

"We can open a bottle of wine. Sit in front of that impressive fire you have going."

"Don't make fun of my fire."

"Just admiring it."

"You can build the next one."

We sit side by side on the sofa with Biscuit in between us.

"Biscuit likes your fires."

"At least somebody does."

"I like your fires."

"But..."

"But when I was growing up, my dad would have my hide if I burned up all the firewood in one week."

"I guess that could be a problem."

"You don't have to worry about it. Wyatt can bring you more."

"So Wyatt's in charge of the firewood?"

"For the most part."

"It doesn't seem fair to the trees." She gets up, grabs a poker, and adjusts the logs.

"In our defense, we plant more trees than we cut down."

"And that keeps people in jobs."

"Exactly."

"I'm just doing my part." I put the poker down and sit back down next to Biscuit. Clasp my hands in my lap. Then reach over and scratch Biscuit's ears. "I'm not used to doing nothing."

"We're not doing nothing," he says.

"How do you figure that?" I ask, cutting my eyes in his direction.

"We're taking a mental health moment."

"A mental health moment. I like it."

"It's very important. And. We're monitoring the fire."

I've noticed that Bradley is quite good at justifying things when he wants to.

"Claire said something that struck me as a bit odd today."

"Yeah? What did Claire say?"

Bradley stretches out his legs and gets comfortable.

"She just said something about Theodore. She said he had a brother."

"Theodore? He didn't have any relatives. Just Thomas."

"Are you sure? She seemed pretty certain."

"I think we would have known about it if he did."

"Maybe." I lean back against the sofa and close my eyes. After a moment, I open my eyes and look into Brandon's light blue eyes. "You don't think there will be any problem, do you?"

"With you being here? No. You're all legal. Signed, sealed, and delivered."

"I hope you're right." When she'd said it, it had sent a little chill through me. Like maybe something wasn't right. It had made me want to check my account again. To make sure the money was still there. But since I'd just checked it that morning before she got here, I didn't do it.

Claire could be wrong about that. And even if she wasn't wrong, like Bradley said, everything was sewn up, all legal like.

Bradley

EVEN THOUGH I'M a hard worker and I don't normally sit still like this either, with Audrey it doesn't seem like we're wasting time.

We make hot chocolate and sit in front of the fireplace.

Her impressive fires are starting to grow on me. Nice and cozy on this unseasonably cool evening.

"To new beginnings," I say, holding up my mug.

"To just breathing," she says, holding up her own mug.

The glow from the fire dances in her eyes, and for a second, I forget what I was going to say.

She leans back on the couch, one leg curled beneath her. "What are you thinking?" she asks, her voice barely above a whisper.

I hesitate. Then tell the truth. "That I want to stay right here."

Audrey holds my gaze, and the air shifts. Warmer. Swirling with something unspoken. Her lips part slightly, like maybe she's thinking about what she wants to say next. Like maybe she doesn't quite know what to say.

Lowering her gaze, she takes a sip of her hot cocoa and I decide she's not going to say anything. We sit quietly, the fire crackling. Biscuit snoring softly.

"I used to think I had everything figured out," she says softly. "Career. Plans. All neat and tidy. And then life said, 'this isn't it.'"

I nod, understanding more than I want to admit.

"Turns out... slowing down isn't the same as giving up," I say.

She takes a deep breath and her siren green eyes lock onto mine. Eyes that I want to tumble into and never come out of.

"How did you get so wise?" she asks.

"I'm not wise." I take a sip of cocoa. "There was a time. When I was young. About the time I was graduating high school." A log falls, sending up a flurry of embers.

"When I wanted to get out of Whiskey Springs. I wanted to see the world."

"What happened?"

"I saw the world."

A little smile plays about her lips. "That's rather vague."

"I spent four years at Purdue getting a degree in engineering."

"You have a degree in engineering?" she asks.

"Don't look so surprised. But. Yes. I do."

"And you came back here."

"After I worked a year at a factory as an engineer. Again. Slowed down. Didn't give up. My family is here. We have a thriving business. I realized I'd rather spend my days working for myself than earning money to make someone else wealthy."

"That makes a lot of sense."

"Here. When I make decisions, they impact something I'm building for my family. I'm building generational wealth."

Biscuit opens his eyes and points his ears forward. Audrey scratches them.

She nods slowly. "None of you are married yet. And no children?"

"I always figured I had plenty of time."

"You said that in the past tense."

Biscuit sits up. Looking toward nothing in particular. But then...

A loud bang.

The sound jolts us both. A sharp, metallic clatter against the porch railing.

With a loud bark, Biscuit jumps off the sofa and heads toward the front door.

Audrey bolts upright. "What was that?"

Biscuit stands at the door, barking. Biscuit has several different barks and this is one I've never heard before. It's vicious and unforgiving.

I'm already moving, pulse thudding. I cross the room in three strides and press my forehead ahead against the window.

Lightning flashes, illuminating the porch for a heartbeat.

Nothing.

But my eyes catch something just beyond the edge of the steps. A shape—maybe a figure—there and gone in the flicker of light.

"Someone's out there," I say, voice low.

Audrey rises slowly, her mug of hot cocoa forgotten on the coffee table. "Are you sure?"

Another crack of thunder answers for me.

I unlock the front door, but only open it a sliver. Biscuit presses forward, growling now, ears rigid, her entire body tense.

Rain lashes the porch, and wind pushes against the door.

I don't see anyone.

But I feel it. Something is off. Like the storm brought more than just wind and rain.

"I'll check it out," I say, even though every instinct screams to keep the door shut.

Audrey's hand grips my arm. "Don't."

Her voice is soft. Frightened.

"It's okay," I say.

I hesitate, then pull the door open just enough to step outside.

The rain hits instantly. Cold, sharp needles against my skin. Biscuit stays behind, pacing at the threshold but unwilling to leave Audrey.

Lightning flashes again.

There's nothing on the steps, but when I glance to the right, toward the side of the porch, I spot it.

A small box. About the size of a bracelet box. Square. Black. Sitting dead center on the porch floor, obviously left there on purpose.

I glance around, heart hammering. Still no sign of anyone.

I reach for it, half-expecting it to be hot or maybe to explode, but it's just a box. I hold it away at arm's length, expecting something to jump out. A spider. A snake.

But inside, there is just a single note lying there. Just a note.

Rain dots the paper as I open it, the ink already smudging.

You shouldn't be here. You were never part of the plan.

I replace the note and slide the box into my pocket.

With one last glance around, I turn and go back inside, securing the door behind me.

"What is it?" Audrey asks, trembling. "What did you see?"

I look into her eyes, haunted again, and everything inside me screams at me not to tell her.

CHAPTER
THIRTY

Audrey

He hesitates. Just for a second. But I feel the shift.

Something clenches in my stomach, instinct maybe, or dread.

"Nothing," he says too quickly. "Just the wind knocking something over."

He won't meet my eyes. That tells me more than his words ever could.

Besides, there's nothing out there to knock over.

I nod anyway. Pretend to believe him. Pretend I don't see the tension in his shoulders or the way his hand stays tucked deep in his pocket like he's holding onto something that might vanish.

"It's getting worse out there," he adds, flipping the deadbolt. "Let's stay away from the windows."

I drift back to the hearth, settling near the warmth though it doesn't quite reach the chill inside me. Outside, the storm howls like something alive. The rain lashes the windows in bursts, each gust louder than the last.

"I didn't know it was going to rain."

"It's like that sometimes up here," he says distractedly, standing next to me in front of the fire.

"You don't think someone's out there, do you?" I ask quietly.

He doesn't answer. Doesn't even look at me. Just stares into the flames like the answers are buried in the embers.

A beat passes. Two.

"No," he says finally.

"What is it?" I ask, with a glance toward his pocket where he still has his hand.

With a sigh, he pulls his hand out of his pocket. He's holding a black box, cheap cardboard faded with rain splatter. Hands it to me.

"What is this?" I ask, looking from the box up to him.

"It was outside."

I instinctively hold it at arm's length.

"I opened it," he adds. "It's a note."

I set it down on the coffee table and drop onto the couch in front of it.

"Why is this happening?"

"Are you going to read it?"

"Did you read it?"

"When I opened it, I couldn't help but read it."

I nod. He's mistakenly worried about my privacy.

"What does it say?"

Getting the idea that I don't want to touch it, he opens the box and holds it up.

You shouldn't be here.
You were never part of the plan.

"What does that mean?" I ask, searching his light blue eyes.

"Hell if I know." He runs a hand along the back of his neck. "But I don't like it."

"Are they talking about me or you?" I wonder.

"Good question."

"With no answer."

"I don't think you should stay here. Until we figure this out."

A trill of panic runs through me. "What do you mean?"

"Someone just threatened you."

"Or you." But now I know what he really thinks. He

thinks the threat is toward me, not him. "Why would someone threaten me? What did I do?"

"I don't know why. Maybe it has something to do with the inheritance."

"But... why?"

"I think you should pack a bag and come stay with me until we find out who's doing this."

I stop, my mug halfway to my lips. "I can't do that."

"I have an extra bedroom."

"No. It's not that. I can't let someone run me away from the house. I won't."

A crash of thunder splits the air overhead, but it sounds like it's moved off a little bit more than it was.

Why would someone come out in the middle of a thunderstorm to leave me a threatening note?

"Did you see anyone outside?"

"I thought I saw a shadow, but I can't be sure. I was pitch dark."

"What do we do? Do we call the sheriff?"

"We can, but... I think we're on our own on this one."

"He wouldn't help us with the flowers?"

Bradley shakes his head, his lips in a thin line.

I lean back against the couch and close my eyes.

"Was there anyone you think might have followed you here from Houston?" he asks, sitting next to me.

"No. Why would they?"

"I don't know. I'm just looking for some kind of explanation."

"I know." I lower my head, covering my face with my hands. "I'm not sure there is one."

"I think the storm is about out of here," he says. "Feel like riding into town? Get a pizza?"

"Seriously?" I ask.

"It's not like we can do anything here."

"You're right." I take a deep breath. "Okay."

Sitting here while someone drops threatening messages off at my front door isn't helping anything. I refuse to cower in fear.

THIRTY-ONE

Bradley

THE STORM MOVES out as quickly as it moved in.

Audrey and I head outside to my truck to go into town to get a pizza.

And I need time to think about what we need to do next.

We both look around as we cross the porch. I don't see any tire tracks. No footprints.

Nothing in the faint glow of the fading sunlight. Nothing to indicate anyone was here.

"Everything smells so good," Audrey says, taking a deep breath. "The spruce trees. Just wow."

I open the passenger door and hold it while she climbs inside.

I don't like the thought of her being up here by herself. It's a beautiful place. Always has been. But that has nothing to do with it.

Under normal circumstances I would think that she's perfectly safe up here, barring a bear or a mountain lion or something nature-related.

It was bad enough that someone had left flowers in her house. That was ambiguous enough that it could be interpreted as several different things. Someone with a key who didn't know she was home as one of the most likely things.

But this note appearing on her porch in the middle of a thunderstorm. An obviously threatening note. That was something else entirely.

No ambiguity. Clearly a threat to her.

I can't make her leave. It's her home. I can't force her to stay with me or even in the lodge, something I haven't brought up yet. I can only appeal to her good sense and logic.

The storm left the air feeling fresh and clean. And like Audrey said, it smells good.

The road from my house up to hers is a dirt road that was never paved.

There's an area of the road just before my house on the way to town that I always consider to be exceptionally precarious. Between Audrey's house and mine.

It's only a few yards, but there are no guardrails. It's an area that I avoid driving during any kind of inclement weather, especially when there's no visibility. It would be far too easy to slide off the edge of the road and there's nothing there but a bottomless slide into the canyon.

I always considered it fortunate that it's a direction I didn't have to travel from my cabin to get into town.

But now I'm wondering if there's a way to add guardrails. Since I'm more of a mechanical engineer than a civil engineer, I don't know the ins and outs of how someone would go about adding guardrails. What I do know, however, is where to find someone who does know.

Just on the other side of that particular area, there is a large curve just before my cabin.

"Is that Claire's car?" Audrey asks, leaning forward in her seat.

I slow down as we pass Claire's old blue Nissan Sentra sitting in a wide place in the dirt road. "It is Claire's car," I say, pulling up behind it. "She must've had car trouble."

"Is she in there?"

"Probably. Wait here. I'll go see."

I climb out of the truck and walk over to the driver's side of Claire's car. She isn't in there, but her purse is on the passenger seat and her cell phone is on the dash.

If she had to get out and walk why would she leave her phone here?

Scratching my head, I walk around the perimeter of

the car, looking for her. I don't see any signs of her or any damage to her car.

Perplexed, I go back to my truck.

"Is she in there?"

"No. I don't see her."

I check my phone and just as I knew I wouldn't, I don't have any cell phone service right here. "Do you have any cell service?"

Audrey checks her phone. "No. This must be a dead zone."

"I'm going to drive down a ways. Call the sheriff."

"Should we look for her?"

"It's going to be dark in a few minutes. The sheriff needs to send out a search and rescue team."

"The whole time we were sitting in front of the fire, she was out here. We could have helped her."

"We couldn't have known."

As I drive the distance down to my house, I can't help but wonder about Claire and the black box with the threatening note.

Had she gotten out of her car and walked back to leave the box on Audrey's porch? Then maybe something happened to her on the way back to her car? I didn't want to think that about Claire, but I couldn't rule it out.

And right now, it was looking like the most likely possibility. The only possibility.

THIRTY-TWO

Audrey

"I FEEL guilty having dinner while Claire is out there."

I'm sitting across from Bradley at a little pizza parlor on Main Street.

The booths have worn blue leather seats. Blue and white checked painted table tops. Everything looks worn, but clean.

There's an outside seating area with heaters, but everyone is sitting inside. All but one of the tables is filled.

A man in a white apron stands in the kitchen, kneading pizza dough. A young woman chops vegetables while an older woman puts on toppings and slides the pizzas into a brick oven.

They make everything from scratch and it smells so good it makes me realize I'm hungrier than I thought I was.

"She could have gotten a ride with someone."

I shake my head. "You said she left her phone and her purse."

"That part I don't understand," Bradley admits. "But Claire can be a little scatterbrained sometimes."

"She does tend to get caught up in whatever she's doing. She didn't even bring her phone inside the house while she worked."

"The older generation isn't quite as attached to their phones as we are."

"I guess." I'm not so sure about that. My parents don't go anywhere without their phones. It obviously depends on the person.

"Are you sure there's nothing we can do?"

"Search and rescue is out there. Doing their thing. If they need volunteers, they'll send out messages calling for them."

I nod. He's right of course. The last thing search and research needs is someone like me getting out there and getting myself into trouble. Then I'd have to be rescued. A more likely than not situation.

I can navigate my way around the city of Houston, but out here, no a chance.

"I just feel bad."

"It's not your fault."

"She'd just left my house. I can't help but feel bad."

"That's because you're such a kind and caring person."

A young lady in jeans and a blue t-shirt that matches the rest of the motif stops at our booth. "Welcome to the pizzeria. Can I take your order?" Her hair is pulled back in a perky ponytail.

"I think we're still deciding," Bradley says, picking up a menu. "Can we get a couple of cokes?"

"Sure thing. Take your time."

"Do you want something stronger?" Bradley asks. "A beer?"

"Not right now. I want to keep a clear head. There's too much going on."

"I agree. What kind of pizza do you like?"

"Pepperoni and pineapple."

He doesn't even bat an eye. "Sounds good." He closes the menu. "They'll find her. I'm sure there's a logical explanation."

"Right." Just like there's a logical explanation for why someone left a threatening note on my porch.

Whatever is happening, it's left me feeling disconcerted.

"There's another option," Bradley says after the waitress comes back and he places our order.

"Please tell me what that would be."

He smiles a little. "You could stay at the Whiskey Springs Lodge. Just until we figure out who's doing this."

I shake my head. "Somebody's trying to run me off and I'm not going. Just because I'm not there for a few days won't make it stop."

He takes a deep breath. Lets it out slowly. Unfortunately you're probably right."

"I won't leave the house. The inheritance stipulates that I live in the house."

He looks perplexed. "For how long?"

"I'm not sure. Forever?"

"That sounds unusual. What happens if you leave?"

"I'm not leaving."

"I understand that." He leans forward. "Hypothetically. Let's say you live there until you're a hundred years old. What happens to the house then?"

"I didn't ask. Maybe it goes to my children."

"Seems likely," he says, sitting back, obviously deep in thought.

Our pizza arrives and our conversation veers away from the stipulations of my inheritance.

But now he has me worried.

I'm just glad he's here to help me navigate all this.

I could tell my sisters, but they already worry too much about me.

It's better that I don't tell them.

CHAPTER
THIRTY-THREE

Bradley

"We're stopping at your cabin?" Audre asks as I pull into the parking space next to my cabin.

"I just need to grab a few things. Some dog food for Biscuit. A change of clothes."

"Why?" she asks, her brow furrowed.

I pause, my hand on the doorknob.

It's dark outside now, but the moon is bright, streaming down in little patches between the trees. There's no sign of the storm that passed through earlier.

"Because if you won't leave your house, then that doesn't give me much choice."

"I don't understand."

"I can't leave you there in your house by yourself."

She looks at me as though I've lost my mind. "Wait," she says. "You're going to stay at my house?"

"Yes." I suppose I should have asked her. "Are you okay with that?"

"I don't know."

"While you're thinking about it, do you want to come inside?"

"I think I'll just sit here."

I really don't like leaving her out here by herself. Not after Claire disappeared from her car. But. I don't want to push her too far.

"Lock the doors." I climb out of the car. I'd feel better if Biscuit was in the truck, at least, but we'd left him at Audrey's house while we went into town for pizza.

"I'll be okay," she insists.

"I won't be long."

I hurry. I grab a bag of Biscuit's dog food. His water bowl. A pair of pajamas I've never worn and a change of clothes. Stow them in an overnight bag.

I toss a toothbrush and a razor into my toiletries bag.

I'm in and out in five minutes.

And yet when I come out of the house and see Audrey sitting there, I feel unimaginable relief.

All my protective instincts are zeroed in on this girl.

"Back," I say tossing my things in the backseat.

"You really don't have to do this."

"I know." I put the truck in reverse.

"I can just go into my bedroom and lock the door at night. That's what I've been doing."

My foot on the break, I look over at her. "Since when?"

"Since someone left those flowers."

I pull out onto the road, headlights lighting the way on the dirt road through the trees. "You shouldn't have to do that in your own house."

She shrugs. I need new door locks."

"Yes. You do." But I wonder. I wonder if even that would make her feel safe in her own home, especially after tonight.

Claire's car is still parked where we left it and another truck, one I recognize as a rescue vehicle, parked behind it.

"They still haven't found her," Audrey points out the obvious.

I pull up in front of her house and kill the motor.

We both look around before we get out. Looking for shadows in the moonlight. Anything that looks out of place.

This is no way to live.

I don't know how to fix it. Not yet. But I will.

I don't have a choice.

THIRTY-FOUR

Audrey

BRADLEY and I stand on the back deck, watching Biscuit make his evening rounds. It's apparently a whole ritual. First the perimeter, nose to the ground like a tiny hound on a mission. Then, once he's satisfied everything smells the way it should, he finally takes care of business.

"He doesn't run away?" I ask.

He shakes his head. "He hasn't yet."

"If he did... if he chased something..." I don't finish the thought.

Bradley glances over, one eyebrow raised like he hears more in my voice than I meant to give away.

"He'd probably get a little lost," he says. "But I think he'd circle back. Eventually."

I nod, even though I'm not sure we're still talking about Biscuit.

The cool air slides between us. I rub my hands together, suddenly unsure what I'm doing out here. On this deck, in this town, standing next to a man who sees too much and says too little.

Still, I stay. Bradley draws me in without meaning to. Soft and steady like a tide I'm not sure I can fight.

He doesn't push. Just stands there with his hands in his pockets and keeps his eyes on Biscuit, who's now pawing at a spot in the grass like he's unearthing treasure.

"You cold?" he asks after a minute.

"A little." I'm actually shivering, but I'm not ready to go back inside.

He shrugs off his leather jacket and drops it over my shoulders. It smells like spruce and campfire. Solid. Warm from his body heat. I wrap it around me. Hesitating, then shrug my arms into the sleeves. It's big, the sleeves covering my hands.

"Thanks," I murmur.

He leans on the railing, quiet again. The kind of silence that doesn't demand to be filled. The kind of silence that is rare.

"I used to think I knew where I belonged," I say before I can stop myself. "Now... I'm not sure."

Bradley doesn't look at me. Just says, "Sometimes it takes losing everything to figure out what home really means." His voice is steady.

I glance at him, but he still isn't looking at me. It makes it easier somehow to talk to him. Too easy.

Maybe that's why I'm able to keep going. Why the words just tumble out of my mouth. Words that I don't even really know where they come from. "I didn't just lose him. I lost who I was with him."

This time he turns and looks at me with those eyes that seem to see everything without asking anything. Our eyes hold, and I feel a magnetic tug. A soft kind of tug that hums deep in my heart. The kind that slips in past the constant ache of pain and emptiness that lives there.

And then Biscuit barks, breaking the spell as he races toward the porch.

Bradley grins. "His highness is finished."

I laugh. A real laugh. One that loosens one of those balls of stress knotted in my stomach.

Inside, the house feels warmer. Softer, even, with the quiet hum of the heater and the faint scent of cinnamon from whatever Claire had done earlier. Biscuit trots in like he lives there, makes two circles by the couch, then flops down in front of the fireplace, obviously choosing his bed for the night.

Bradley grabs his overnight bag from the foyer and glances upstairs, then back at me. "Which guest room do you want me in?" He asks it like it's the most natural thing in the world.

"The one next to mine is already made up," I say, gesturing toward the stairs. "Clean sheets."

He smiles, but there's a question in it. One he doesn't quite ask.

I turn to fill the kettle with water, needing something warm to calm my nerves. "You'll be comfortable. It's quiet up there."

"Quiet's good," he says, then walks away with slow, deliberate steps. At the bottom of the stairs, he pauses. "Thanks for letting me stay."

I glance over, the steam from the kettle curling between us. "You're welcome. It's not like you gave me much of a choice."

His eyes hold mine for a moment longer than they should. Then he nods and disappears up the stairs, his footsteps muffled on the carpeted landing.

I let out a breath I hadn't realized I was holding.

Behind me, Biscuit snores softly on the floor near the hearth. I pour two mugs of tea, then hesitate. One or two?

I set both on the coffee table anyway.

Just in case.

THIRTY-FIVE

Bradley

I set my toiletries bag on the bathroom counter. Like the closets in this house, the bathrooms could do with some updates. I probably wouldn't gut them like the Bentley cabin bathrooms, but definitely some updates.

A new sink. New countertop. New faucet.

I pull back the shower curtain. New tub and shower.

Okay. Maybe I would gut this bathroom, too, and start over.

But it's not my decision to make.

I splash some water on my face and brush my teeth.

Maybe I shouldn't have pushed myself in on Audrey like this.

My being worried about her doesn't give me the right to just take over her life.

She was right. I hadn't given her much of a choice.

I need to apologize to her.

I head back downstairs to see if she's still up.

She's sitting on the sofa, her feet pulled up beneath her, two mugs of hot tea on the coffee table.

The only light comes from the fireplace.

My heart warms. She made me tea.

But then I see her face.

She's holding her phone.

"What's wrong?" I ask, sitting next to her.

Her eyes look haunted again as she meets my gaze.

She glances down at her phone.

"Someone named Mr. Fields called me."

"Who's that?"

"I don't know. He runs an agency that hires the people who take care of the house. He's the one who pays Claire."

"What did he want?"

"They found her. They found Claire."

"Is she okay?" Her expression already tells me she isn't.

"I don't know. They're taking her into Denver to the hospital."

"What else did he say?"

She pulls her gaze away from mine. "Just that they found her. She was unconscious."

I pick up one of the mugs. Press it into her hands. "She'll be okay. They were able to find her. That's a good thing."

"I hope so." She holds the mug up to her chin, breathing in the steam. "Do you think the same person who left the note hurt her?"

"I don't know. Maybe she can tell us what happened when she wakes up."

"Right."

"Is this mine?" I nod toward the other mug of tea.

"If you want it."

"Thank you." I pick up the mug and take a sip of the hot tea.

"You're welcome." She looks at me a moment. "You've never heard of Mr. Fields?"

"No."

"I thought you knew everyone in town."

"I did, too."

"Claire told me she has an app. That she has to log in when she gets here and log out when she leaves. That there's an agency she works for."

"I'll see what I can find out about it. Tomorrow."

"Okay."

"It's been a busy day. Let's just relax for a moment and enjoy this fire."

"It's not a very good one," she says, keeping a straight face.

"I agree. We've got to get it up to your standards." I get up and step over Biscuit to add another log to it.

"Biscuit is definitely relaxed," she says.

"It's a gift."

A smile plays about her lips and she glances toward the windows. A wall of darkness that we can't see past.

"We'll measure those windows tomorrow," I say.

She looks at me, her eyes wide. "I know I didn't say it, but I'm glad you're here."

"Me too." I sit back down next to her.

My gaze locks onto hers and she doesn't look away.

My heart thuds in my chest.

She's right beside me, close enough that her shoulder almost brushes mine. But not quite.

I could shift. Just a little.

But I don't.

Her gaze holds mine. Something unsure and unspoken flickering behind her eyes.

The soft firelight casts golden shadows across her face, catching in her hair. She looks like something I might have dreamed of once. When I was younger and life was simpler.

"I should head up," she whispers, but she doesn't move.

"Yeah," I say, even though I don't want her to.

She sips her tea and we sit there a few moments longer. Not touching. Not speaking.

Just feeling.

Finally, she stands up with a slow reluctance. "Goodnight, Bradley."

"Goodnight," I say.

She seems like she wants to say more.

Instead, she just nods, her gaze lingering a moment longer before she turns toward the hallway.

I wait until I hear her door click shut before I breathe again.

Biscuit shifts a bit from his spot in front of the fire, utterly at peace.

I wish I could say the same about myself.

THIRTY-SIX

Audrey

I WAKE the next morning to bright sunlight streaming in through my slightly cracked window.

It's so quiet. So peaceful. I have to listen carefully to hear the faint sound of the river in the distance. Birds singing their morning song. The breeze rustling through the aspen trees.

My first thought is Bradley. Wondering if he's still here.

I stretch beneath the warm blankets as the cold morning breeze drifts in through the window along with the sunlight.

I quickly replay the events of yesterday, my thoughts slowing as I come to last night.

That moment when Bradley and I had sat next to each other on the sofa, Biscuit snoring at our feet, all of us enjoying the warmth of the fireplace.

Bradley's light blue eyes had latched onto mine and held. So much warmth and kindness there. So much understanding.

Too much understanding.

It's only been three weeks since I'd become a widow. I'm still trying to adjust.

Should be still trying to adjust.

I think finding out Thomas wasn't who I thought he was had dulled some of the shininess off our marriage. Thomas and I hadn't known each other all that long and we'd been married even less time.

He'd had a magnetic confidence that I had been drawn to from the beginning.

When he proposed, it had seemed like the natural next step. The right thing to do.

I had been a twenty-six-year-old chasing a future I thought I was supposed to want. He offered all the things I told myself mattered: security, stability, a neat and tidy version of forever.

And he was a pilot. That had dazzled me more than I care to admit. There was something romantic about that. In retrospect, I'd believed that being with him might come with a passport to adventure.

But it turns out, charm like that fades quickly. And the sky always looks bluer from the ground.

I pull myself out of the bed, putting my feet on the cold wooden floor.

As I hurry across the cold floor to the bathroom where I'd left my slippers, it suddenly occurs to me that I can actually afford to have heated floors installed.

I slide my feet into my slippers and turn on the shower to let the water heat up.

I could put in one of those free-standing bathtubs with a separate shower, the showers with more than one shower head. Overhead rain heads and soft sprayers.

I could even put a fireplace in the bathroom.

Not even do I have the money to do it, I have a handsome and attentive neighbor who seems like he's willing and able to do just about anything to the house I can dream up.

Standing in the hot shower, I let the water run down over my head, washing away some of the guilt I'd been feeling at enjoying spending time with Bradley.

Thomas had always worked a lot, spending most of his time at the airport and flying. After we'd gotten married, he'd stepped up his work game even more. We rarely did anything together as a couple. That was probably one of the many reasons I'd felt so isolated out in Katy.

I don't even know if he visited his child downtown. I

worked downtown. Maybe he visited his child and baby momma when I was at home in Katy. I'll never know.

There were so many things I didn't know about him. It doesn't matter now.

My life with Thomas is something I can start putting behind me.

Thomas's grandfather, Theodore Albright, had set me up with this house. I wish I could have met him. He unknowingly changed my life and I'll forever be indebted to him for that.

I turn off the water and step out into the chilly air.

Definitely seriously considering heated floors and a gas fireplace in the bathroom.

Right after the new door locks and window shades. And, of course, the closets.

I kneel on the floor of the bedroom and dig through the clothes in my suitcases. At least everything is organized even if it is still in suitcases.

I decide on a pair of blue jeans and a long t-shirt with a sweatshirt over it. It seems cooler today and cloudy. A nice reprieve from the heat that is currently hanging over Houston.

A little preview of the winter to come. I probably shouldn't be looking forward to winter so much. Bradley seems to think it's a novelty that won't last. Being from here, he would know. But being from here, he might not know just how long I might enjoy the novelty of a winter that includes cold weather and snow.

After getting dressed I spend a little extra time blow drying my hair out straight and smooth, but I don't put on any makeup. Just in case Bradley is still here, I want to appear casual and nonchalant.

Not that I am.

His quiet, protective presence has me feeling alive again.

And now that I'm feeling it, I realize it's been a very, very long time, before Thomas's plane crash even, that I've felt this way.

As soon as I open my bedroom door, I already know he's not here. The house feels quiet and empty.

I find a note written on a sheet of legal paper on the kitchen island.

*Meeting my brother to get some work at the
Bentley place.
Be back later this afternoon.
Call me if you need anything.*

HIS SIMPLE NOTE makes me smile to myself as I make myself a cup of coffee using the fancy coffee maker. I feel ridiculously giddy at the thought that he's coming back this afternoon.

I'm getting far too used to having Bradley around far

too quickly.

He's a friend. It's okay to have a friend.

Even if that friend does have me thinking about what it might feel like to kiss him.

THIRTY-SEVEN

Bradley

"YOU'VE BEEN SPENDING a lot of time over at the widow's house," Wyatt says as we carry a new sink into the Bentley cabin.

"Audrey," I say. "Hold on. Turn it on its side. Going to be spending a lot more time over there, too."

"You don't say." Wyatt gives me a raised eyebrow look.

"Not like that." We carefully set the sink down and start unboxing it.

"Okay then. Why not? And how?"

"I guess you didn't hear about what happened last night."

"I guess I didn't. You going to tell me?"

I pull away the packing material and hand it to Bradley to carry out of the bathroom.

"Do you remember Claire?"

"Claire? I don't think so."

"Older than us. She cleans the Albright house."

"Okay. What happened to her?"

"She went missing right after she left Audrey's house. Left her car on the side of the road. Her phone still in the car. Search and research went out last night looking for her."

"So that what all that commotion was about." We shift the sink into place.

"How do you keep your head in the sand like that?"

"It's easy. I don't bother people and they don't bother me."

"Impressive. At any rate, they found her unconscious. She's in the hospital."

He sits back on his heels. "Besides the obvious tragedy, doesn't that sound a little odd to you?"

"That's not the worst of it. Somebody left a threatening note on Audrey's porch during the rainstorm."

"What kind of threatening note?"

"It said *You shouldn't be here. You were never part of the plan.*"

"What plan?" he asks.

"I don't know, Bro. Something that involves Audrey."

"Or you," he says.

"That's what Audrey said."

"What are you planning on doing?"

"The basics. New locks. Shades on the windows. And..." I measure the sink on either side. Make sure it's even. "I'm staying in the guest room until we find out who's threatening her."

"So you're moving in."

"I didn't say I was moving in. I said I was staying there until we figure out who's threatening her." I say the words slowly, like I would say them to a child.

He responds in kind, his words slow and deliberate. "So you're moving in."

Scowling at my brother, I pick up a wrench. Point it at him. "It's not like that."

He shrugs. "Whatever you say."

"Let's get this sink installed so we can get out of here. I've got to install new door locks on Audrey's doors."

Wyatt sits back on his heels and smirks at me.

THIRTY-EIGHT

Audrey

"What are you smiling about?" Brianna asks before I'd hardly done more than answer her FaceTime call.

"I'm not smiling," I say, biting my lip because that was exactly what I was doing.

"What are you doing?" Brianna asks.

"I'm building a fire." I'm on my knees in front of the fireplace getting a fire going.

"I rather figured that," she says. "You have smut on your face."

"Oh." I swipe at my cheek to get the smut off.

Brianna laughs out loud.

"What?" I squint at my own reflection in the smaller part of the screen.

"You look like Cinderella."

Smiling, I sit back on my heels. "Why aren't you at work?"

"I am at work." She pans her phone behind her at the shelves loaded with books.

"What job is this one?" I ask. Brianna is currently working at a temp agency and even though she's had lot of offers for full-time jobs, she likes the novelty of working at different offices. I think she also secretly likes the lower sense of responsibility that comes with being temporary.

"It's for a publishing company. I like it."

"You like everything as long as it's temporary."

She shrugs, but doesn't say one way or the other.

"I think our parents must have messed us up pretty bad."

"Why do you say that?" Brianna frowns into the phone.

"Well. You don't have a full-time job—"

"I work full-time."

"Yes. But not at any one particular place doing anything in particular."

"I'm an office assistant."

"Brianna." I take a breath. "Never mind."

"I get it. Go ahead. Finish what you're trying to say."

"I was just going to say that you work for a temp

agency." *Because you decided not to go to law school.* "Lilah works as a bartender because she wants to be an artist. And I..." I wave a hand in no particular direction.

"I thought you liked working at the art gallery," Brianna says.

"I didn't hate it."

"But it wasn't your career of choice."

"No. It wasn't."

"Well. It's okay. Because now you don't have to work."

"I'm going to start looking for a job after I get the house together."

"Are you still working on the closets?"

"How did you know about the closets?" I poke at the fire, sending embers up the chimney.

"Lilah told me."

"Of course. Yes. I'm still working on the closets."

"You're never going to finish working on that house."

I sigh. "I know. But I am going to start looking for work."

"I wouldn't. You've got plenty of money. You can do whatever you want to do."

"Maybe whatever I want to do is to work. Don't give me that look. I need purpose."

"Hey. Who am I to judge?"

"Why are you calling me from work anyway?"

"I wanted to talk to you about Lilah."

"What's wrong with Lilah?"

"I think you need to talk to her."

CHAPTER

THIRTY-NINE

Bradley

I STOP BY MY HOUSE. Shower. Pack a fresh set of clothes for tomorrow. Wash a couple of dishes I'd left in the sink. All the while keeping an eye on Biscuit as he surveys his yard.

I have no doubt that Biscuit thinks the yard is his domain. It might as well be. He knows every crook and cranny better than I ever will.

I bring in the mail. Go through it, tossing ninety percent of it in the trash.

Since Wyatt's words are stuck in my head, I take my time. Doing the things I would normally do at my house when I get home from work.

I usually either go into town for something to eat or throw something in the oven. Maybe the microwave.

But I know I'm not doing that tonight. I'm heading over to Audrey's as soon as can justify it. I have to feel like I'm spending enough time here at my place that I don't feel like I'm living at Audrey's.

I can't stand the thought of Wyatt being right. Just because he's Wyatt. And he thinks he's smarter than he is.

Audrey said something that has me wondering. Something that I don't quite understand. It sort of just slid past me at the time, but I keep coming back to it.

She said she *can't* leave. That the inheritance stipulates she live in the house to keep it. I can't stop wondering what's so important that she has to stay in the house.

Still mulling that over, I grab a beer from my refrigerator and take it outside with me.

It's been a cold, dreary day all day. Now it's a cold, dreary evening.

Clouds are gathered around the mountain peaks. Probably snowing up there. The weather is definitely keeping the hikers on lower ground today, doubtless making the shop owners on Main Street happy.

As soon as I open the beer, sit down on a chair on my back deck, Biscuit sits down in front of me. Looks east toward Audrey's house. Then look back at me and barks once.

"There is no way you're that damn smart."

Biscuit barks again. Just one bark.

"Okay," I say. "It's not like we're doing anything here anyway, is it?"

Biscuit stands up and wags his tail.

I water a little rock garden next to my deck with what was almost a full bottle of beer.

"Come on Biscuit. Let's go toss everything into the truck and see what Audrey's up to."

Biscuit follows me inside and waits at the front door while I gather everything up.

I no more than get the truck door open than he's inside, ready to go.

Someone moved Claire's car. Good. That means I don't have to deal with it.

I'm actually not too interested in getting involved with anything that looks like foul play. And what happened to Claire definitely hints of foul play. Whether by her or by someone else, I don't have any way of knowing.

She doesn't seem like the kind of person that would leave threatening messages on someone's doorstep. But then I really don't know anything about her. She's not originally from Whiskey Springs. I don't know how long she's lived here, but some people always seem to hover on the outside, never really becoming part of the community. She's one of those people.

I pull up to the front of Audrey's house and cut the motor.

It didn't take much time for this to start feeling more like home than my own place.

Just goes to show. A home isn't just a house.

A home is a place where a person feels welcome and it's more like a home if someone lives there that we care about.

I've found that place here. With Audrey.

Unfortunately, due to the very circumstances that got her here, I can't tell her that. It's too soon.

She came to Whiskey Springs to heal. Not to get caught up in a romantic entanglement.

It's going to take all the willpower I have to keep that in the forefront of my mind.

She throws the door open before I'm more than halfway across the porch.

"I'm so glad you're here," she says. "I need to show you something."

CHAPTER

FORTY

Audrey

AFTER I GET off the phone with Brianna, I leave a message for Lilah to call me back.

Since she works all hours of the night at a bar, she sleeps all hours of the day.

I don't see how she does it. Mornings are my best time of day. I like watching the wonder of the sunrise. The way the sky pinkens ever so slowly. How just looking away for a few minutes and the whole landscape changes.

How the sky is like nature's mandala, especially early in the morning. So far, since I've gotten here, I haven't gotten up early enough to truly appreciate the sunrise, but I will.

I spend the rest of my morning, after talking to my sister, playing around with closet designs using a pad of graph paper I found on the desk Theodore had used. The desk is tucked away beneath the stairs in a space that will make a cute little office area. I make a mental note to fix it up for myself to do whatever it is I decide to do for work.

I'm thinking maybe I'll try to work from home. If the winters are as bad as I have a feeling they're going to be, I don't want to be driving to work every day.

When the lead on the one pencil I have breaks, I go in search of another pencil.

Someone must have cleaned out the desk, taking Theodore's personal papers with them.

Not finding another pencil and not wanting to drive into town just to buy a pencil, for God's sake, I look through his desk drawers.

It feels a little invasive at first, but I remind myself that it's my desk now. The house and everything in it is mine.

When I go to open the top left hand drawer, an obvious place for pencils if you ask me, I find it locked.

There's no key anywhere to be found. Not in the ceramic tray on the top of the desk or any of the unlocked drawers.

After a moment's hesitation, I pick up a letter opener

and work on manually using it for a key to unlock the drawer.

I am a woman on a mission. Finding a pencil or even a pencil sharpener doesn't sound like too much to ask.

Turns out the desk is old and the lock isn't very sophisticated.

I'm able to open it right up with the letter opener. Unfortunately there is no pencil inside. How could the man not have more than one pencil?

What I do find is something unexpected.

A folded envelope, yellowed at the edges, sealed with wax in an old-fashioned manner, but someone used the letter opener to slit the top of it open. No return address. Just the name Theodore Albright scrawled across the front in bold, slanted handwriting.

My pulse skips.

Time seems to slow down, moving in slow motion as I sit back in the old wooden office chair that creaks with age.

I shouldn't read it. I know I shouldn't. Could this have something to do with Theodore's brother Claire spoke of?

I let out a sigh and do it.

Inside is a single sheet of paper. No date. No signature. Just a few lines written in a hurried hand:

Theodore,
We agreed to keep quiet while you were getting

things in order. But time is running out, and you know he deserves better than being erased. I know you think she won't understand, but she's stronger than you give her credit for.

You can't change what happened, but you can at least make it right.

If this goes to probate without his name in the file, I won't stay silent. You know I kept the records.

— J

My breath catches.

I stare at the letter, my stomach twisting.

Who is being erased?

And make what right?

I glance over my shoulder even though I know I'm alone.

For now.

Oddly enough, the letter was the only thing in the locked desk drawer.

I'm still sitting at the desk, the letter laid out in front of me when Bradley drives up.

The relief I feel is unsettling in itself.

Bradley is staying with me for now but I can't count on him staying here for long.

After the novelty wears off... after time passes and we don't find out who's leaving the threatening notes, he'll go back to his own life. Want to sleep in his own bed.

It's understandable.

For the moment, however, I'm just happy to see him.

"I need to show you something," I say, throwing open the door.

FORTY-ONE

Bradley

"I'm pretty sure I have a pencil in my truck," I tell Audrey as she explains why she went exploring in Theodore's desk.

We're sitting in front of the fireplace, with Biscuit on the floor in his new favorite place, and she's holding a yellowed folded envelope with an old wax seal.

"It's okay," she says. "It's not about the pencil... but I'll take it. Later. It's about what I found in the desk."

"I take it you found a letter."

She glances down at the letter in her hands. "Yeah. It was already open so I read it."

"I would have read it if you didn't. What does it say?"

She hands me the letter.

I carefully pull it out of the envelope and read it out loud.

"*Theodore,*

We agreed to keep quiet while you were getting things in order. But time is running out, and you know he deserves better than being erased. I know you think she won't understand, but she's stronger than you give her credit for.

You can't change what happened, but you can at least make it right.

If this goes to probate without his name in the file, I won't stay silent. You know I kept the records.

—J

I look at Audrey. "Who is J?"

"I don't know. Maybe he's the brother Claire mentioned."

"Maybe." He looks back up at me. "Theodore must have read this."

"Someone did."

"It's odd that it was locked away like that."

"Agreed. We might not ever know why." I hand the letter back over to her.

"I don't understand."

"I know. It's troubling." I run a hand along the back of my neck. "Someone questioned what Theodore did."

"I should show it to someone?"

"I don't think so. I think it would just stir up something that's already settled."

"The inheritance."

"It's all settled, right?"

"As far as I know."

"You do what you want. But my advice? Just put it away somewhere."

"Yeah. I think you're right," she says, looking at me with her meadow green eyes. "I'm just worried that it has something to do with that note someone left on my porch."

"Yeah. I'm thinking we just hold onto that, too, for now."

She gives me a skeptical look.

"It's a small town. I don't think the sheriff could do anything."

"It's the same way in the city. Not enough resources. Somebody almost has to get hurt before they'll do anything."

Reaching over, I put a hand on hers. "I won't let that happen. I'm going to stay right here until we find out who's doing this."

"What if we never find out?"

"You sound like Wyatt." I squeeze her hand. "We'll find out."

I know she doesn't believe me. I can see it in her face.

But what she doesn't know is that I don't care how

long it takes. I'm staying right here until whoever is threatening her is held accountable.

"My sister is calling me back," she says, picking up her phone. "I need to take it."

"Sure. Do whatever you need to do."

"Hello," she says into the phone.

"Come on, Biscuit. Let's go take a walk."

Audrey glances over at me with a little smile.

"Is someone there with you?" her sister asks.

"I'll tell you later. Brianna is worried about you."

I step outside into the brisk evening air, Biscuit slipping out ahead of me.

The sun is just sliding down behind the mountains, leaving an early sunset behind. The scent of firewood smoke hovers in the air, settling among the trees.

A couple of chipmunks scamper along the top rail of the deck, then leap onto the limbs of a nearby spruce tree, making a ruckus in the limbs, sending delicate little needles falling to the ground.

I can't help but scan the perimeter, out to the tree line, into the trees, looking for something that doesn't belong. *Someone* who doesn't belong.

Knowing that someone was here leaves everything feeling unsettled and leaves me with a lot of unanswered questions.

Is someone out to harm Audrey? Or just hoping to frighten her away without any intent of harming her?

It's such an ambiguous situation, I don't know if we'll ever have answers.

Audrey and Wyatt are right about that. And what if we don't find out who threatened her and left flowers in her house?

What will I do then?

That remains to be seen. I pick up a twig and toss it. Biscuit surprises me by chasing it bringing it back.

"I didn't know you could do that," I tell him, tossing the twig out again. "Where did you learn these things?"

To my way of thinking, the situation is fluid. It can go so many different ways. Maybe I will have to move in here permanently. Or maybe it will resolve itself. Or maybe Audrey will tire of having me around and send me back to my place.

Right now, she's caught off guard and doesn't know what to think.

How long that will last remains to be seen.

"Hey." Audrey comes to the door.

"Hey. All done?"

"Yeah. She was on her way to work. Couldn't talk. I was thinking about making dinner. Want to help?"

"Sure."

Biscuit races toward the back door as though he understands English.

Following her inside, I lock the door behind us.

This is most definitely getting far too comfortable. Far too fast.

The odd thing about it is that I don't mind.

I don't mind even a little.

Being with Audrey like this feels right.

And if I'm getting used to it, who could blame me?

FORTY-TWO

Audrey

The scent of garlic and oregano fills the kitchen, warm and mouthwatering. Bradley stands at the stove, stirring the simmering pot of spaghetti sauce like it's a sacred ritual. He has a wooden spoon in one hand, a crooked grin on his face, and a dish towel slung over one shoulder.

"This," he says, giving the sauce a slow swirl, "is exactly how I taught my brothers to make it. They were thirteen and fifteen, more interested in burning toast than learning how to properly make a sauce. But. Being the older brother I am, I insisted. I told them, 'One day you'll want to impress a girl, and this is how you'll do it.'"

He turns to look at me then, eyes catching the light just enough to make my stomach flutter.

"Did it work?" I ask, tearing lettuce into the wooden bowl in front of me. "Did they impress a girl?"

He chuckles, the sound low and easy. "Maybe. But I'm not going to guarantee it. Caleb tried adding ketchup once. I didn't speak to him for a week."

I laugh, but the sound caught in my throat. It was suddenly too easy to picture a younger Bradley, patient and bossy, showing his brothers how to stir just right. It was too easy to imagine him like this in other kitchens, with other women. Doing some impressing himself.

"Where was your mother?"

"Outside. In her garden. She taught us how to grow basil and oregano. But she was never much into being in the kitchen. This was after I'd spent the summer with my mother's mother in Boston."

Biscuit thumps his tail against the floor and gives a little huff, flopping beneath the table and rolling to his back, waiting for someone to notice how adorably neglected he is.

"You're spoiled, you know that, right?" I crouch for half a second to scratch him under the chin before turning back to the salad.

Bradley's voice softens behind me. "You ever teach anyone to cook?"

I hesitate, then smile faintly. "Kind of. When we were little, my sisters and I used to pretend we were on a cooking show with our father as the judge. We'd have bake-offs but my super competitive sister, Brianna, tried to sneak hot pepper into our cookie dough."

"Sounds chaotic," he says, his voice soft.

"It was." I look up.

"Maybe chaos is what makes family work."

He's watching me, spoon resting on the counter now. Our eyes lock and something shifts in the air. Something thick and humming and fragile.

He takes a step forward.

I don't breathe.

The world narrows to the space between us, to the way his gaze flicks to my lips and back again. I'm not sure who moved first, only that his hand brushed mine, warm and pleasantly calloused and grounding.

Then the sauce sizzles behind him, spitting onto the stop top with a hiss.

He blinks and turns, muttering a curse as he grabs the spoon again. The moment shattered.

I clear my throat and toss another handful of lettuce into the bowl, pretending I'm not shaking just a little.

"Your brothers seriously owe you," I say, trying for a teasing tone that I'm not feeling. "That sauce smells like it belongs in a five-star restaurant."

He stirs the sauce like he's done it a thousand times. Slow, confident, the wooden spoon scraping in a lazy circle, keeping his gaze on what he's doing. "It was never really about the recipe," he says, voice low, almost too soft to hear over the simmer.

Biscuit gets up and wanders back to his place in front of the fireplace like he belongs here.

I watch the way Bradley's shoulders move, the way his hands guide the spoon. He taught his younger brothers to cook. I've never known another man who did that. A legacy built from tomatoes, garlic, and quiet loyalty. He says it's not about the recipe, but I think it is. Or at least, what it stands for.

He still isn't looking at me.

Maybe it's a good thing. Because if he does, he'll see everything written across my face.

How much I wish I'd known this version of him back then and how much I wish things had been different and I had been part of his life when we were younger.

How much I want to believe it's not too late.

He might even see the hope simmering in my eyes. The hope that he and I can create something together. Now. That it's not too late for either of us.

I clear my throat and look away.

I shouldn't want this. Not yet. Maybe not ever again. But when he looks into my eyes I long for something.

Something I can't even identify yet. Something that swirls into those places deep in my heart that I thought were locked forever.

CHAPTER

FORTY-THREE

Bradley

WHEN I CAME BACK INSIDE from walking Biscuit, Audrey has the table set with a single white tapered candle softly glowing. One salad in front of each of our plates.

"It's my first real meal here." She says with a little shrug before I manage to hide my surprise.

"It's nice," I say. "It's perfect."

Biscuit heads over to his spot in front of the fireplace and curls back up.

Apparently I didn't hide my surprise quickly enough.

"It's too much," she says, picking up the candle and blowing it out. "My head wasn't—"

I reach her in three long strides. Put my hands over hers. "I just wish I'd thought of it. And—"

I put a finger beneath her chin and nudge her face up until her eyes meet mine.

Her eyes are red-rimmed and brimming with tears.

"Oh, sweetheart." I pull her against me, wrapping her in my arms.

She hesitates a second, two, then wraps her arms around me, resting her cheek against my chest.

"You're trembling," I say, pressing my hand against the back of her head, holding her steady.

"I'm okay," she says, her voice muffled against me. "I'm sorry. I just— Everything was just—"

"It's okay." I make little soothing sounds, but she seems to tremble even more.

I just hold her. It's all I can do.

Making dinner with Audrey was so unexpectedly... nice. Normal even. And I've gone and ruined it. Now I've hurt her. She thinks the candles were too much.

But it's not that. It's that they were just so... right.

And I've been telling myself to take it easy. To go slow. That she's a grieving widow.

That I can't make assumptions with her.

She's not a typical woman. She's not someone I can allow myself to get close to.

She's vulnerable and grieving.

My job is to protect her.

Not to want to kiss her like I do.

After a couple of minutes, she stills and lifts her head.

"Can I take this?" I ask, taking the candle she's still holding.

She nods.

I light it and set it in the middle of the table.

"You don't have to..." She runs a hand through her hair, shoving it off her face.

"I want to. Here." I pull out a chair and hold it while she sits. "I'll just fix our plates."

She sits quietly while I stir the sauce, giving a little extra heat, before making our plates.

I'm at a loss as to how to proceed. All I know to do is to act like nothing has changed.

"Now we get to see if I still remember how to make my grandmother's recipe."

"It's been a while since you made it?" she asks.

"To be honest, I haven't made it since I taught my brothers."

She freezes, her fork halfway to her mouth.

"Surely you're kidding with me."

"I'm not."

"So you've never made this to impress a girl?"

"You're the first."

She tilts her head to the side and looks at me with an expression between disbelief and something else. Relief maybe? Hope?

"In case you're wondering," she says. "It works."

FORTY-FOUR

Audrey

"Do you want help with that fire?" I ask.

"It takes a knack to get it up to your standards, but I'll get it."

I'm sitting on the sofa, a glass of wine in hands, my feet tucked up beneath me.

Biscuit, sitting on the floor, and I watch as Bradley gets the fire going. It's actually a very nice, steady fire.

"I think it's okay," I say. "Looks very professional."

"Are you sure?" He sits back on his heels and looks at me over his shoulder. "I don't want you to be disappointed."

"I'm not disappointed."

"Okay." Getting up from where he knelt in front of the hearth, he sits on the couch next to me and picks up his glass of wine.

"Haven't we tried this before?" he asks.

"I think we did, actually." I look toward the wall of dark windows. "Maybe this time we won't have any unwelcome guests."

"Let's hope not."

"What other things did you teach your younger brothers about impressing girls?"

"There's not much." He stretches out his legs. "Besides cooking spaghetti, they had to know how to cook eggs."

"You taught them to cook eggs?"

"Sure."

"I thought cooking eggs was just something all guys knew how to do."

"They have to learn it somewhere."

"You learned from your grandmother."

"That's right. And my grandfather taught me how to build the perfect fire. I still miss them both terribly. Anyway, my brothers weren't interested in learning to build a well-laid fire. Our father had already taught us how to throw one together and they were good with that."

"That explains your well-laid fire."

"What about you? Did you teach your younger sisters anything?"

"Not really. Except I always helped them with their homework."

"Practical and important."

"Underappreciated."

"I think just about anything we try to teach our younger siblings goes underappreciated."

"You might be right. Maybe it's supposed to be that way." I think about my two younger sisters. Both of them so different from the other and both different from me.

"Most people don't suspect we're sisters," I say.

"Really? Maybe it's because we live in a small town, but everyone thinks my brothers and I look alike."

"I don't know. I've only met Wyatt, but he's more rugged looking than you are."

"Rugged is a good thing, right?"

"It can be. It's not better or worse. It's just different."

I don't tell him that I find him more attractive than his brother. There's nothing wrong with Wyatt. Wyatt is a good-looking man.

But there's something about Bradley and his kind light blue eyes that strikes me deep in my core. That makes me feel more alive than I've felt in longer than I can remember.

FORTY-FIVE

Bradley

"I HAVE to be up early in the morning to meet my brother. We're still working out at the Bentley place."

"That's Biscuit's cue to go outside," Audrey says. "And mine to head upstairs.

She takes our two wine glasses, only half empty, to the kitchen.

I round my dog up and take him outside into the brisk night air for his walk.

I try not to think too much about what it means that I'd had such a good time with Audrey. Making dinner.

Sitting in front of the fire. Talking about our siblings and our childhoods.

Both of us being the oldest, we have a lot in common, she and I.

Even though I'm from a small town and she's from the big city, it doesn't seem to matter.

She seems to belong here just as sure as if she was from here.

If she stays, she won't be like Claire, someone who stays on the periphery of the town. She'll be a part of the town, weaving her way into the fabric.

I don't know how I know this. It's just a gut feeling I have about her.

Biscuit finishes his rounds and we head back inside.

A quick glance around tells me that Audrey has already headed upstairs.

Turning off the lights, I follow, heading up to my room. Biscuit chooses to lie down in from of the fireplace and stay downstairs. For now at least. He'll probably be up later.

I stop at Audrey's closed door and listen until I hear water running in the bathroom.

I would have liked to have said goodnight to her.

But maybe it's better this way.

If we'd come upstairs together, I probably would have done something stupid like kiss her.

That wouldn't be fair to her.

She hasn't had time to grieve. As much as I might want her to be something more, she hasn't had time to be in a place to be more.

I put a hand on her doorknob. Turn it. Not to open it, but to see if she locked it. She'd told me that she sleeps in her room with the door locked. But it's not locked.

For whatever reason, she's left it unlocked.

I go into my own room, but I leave the door open. I need to be able to hear anything out of the ordinary. To hear if anyone breaks in. Comes upstairs.

Biscuit is still downstairs, so he's an extra layer of guard dog.

The incident with the candle at dinner was another indication of just how vulnerable Audrey is. She'd lit a candle for a candle light dinner. An innocent gesture. All it had taken was one surprised look from me to reduce her to a trembling wreck.

I can't do that to her. It's not fair.

She deserves time. She came here to take time to heal.

I can't take that away from her.

And yet I don't know how I can be here with her. In the same house and not want more.

How is it possible that she and I can spend time like this together without me wanting to hold her? To kiss her?

To make a life with her?

I have to give her time.

To see what happens next. To be here for her while giving her space.

I never said it would be easy.

It's anything but easy.

FORTY-SIX

Audrey

THE HOUSE FEELS lonely without Bradley and Biscuit.

As I sit out back sipping my first cup of hot coffee, wrapped in a wool blanket because I don't have a coat yet, I consider again getting a dog. Or maybe a cat.

I'm mostly a cat person and we had cats growing up, but a dog seems like the best choice. A dog like Biscuit can come outside with me and a dog is better at scaring off intruders than a cat would be.

It would take an awfully fierce cat to scare anyone off.

I hate it that my gaze is constantly drawn to scan the

perimeter of the area around me. That I can't sit quietly without looking around me, even over my shoulder.

Deciding it's not worth being outside and it's too cold anyway, I take my coffee and go back inside.

The fire in the fireplace died down overnight, making the house now seem cold and dismal. I hope this isn't what winter is going to be like.

I'll have to keep a fire going all the time just to stave off the dreariness. I sit at the breakfast table, the only spot with a little bit of sunshine coming in through the window and finish my coffee. Still watching outside for anything that looks out of place.

There's nothing I can do about that.

I've just finished washing my coffee mug and laying it aside to dry when Lilah FaceTimes me.

"Lilah. What's wrong?" Lilah is usually... always... still sound asleep this time of morning. Probably not even gone to bed by this time a lot of nights.

"I quit my job," she blurts.

"But why? I thought you liked your job."

She scrunches up her face. "Like might be a strong word. More like I tolerated it."

"Oh." This is news to me. But in all fairness, I've been a little self-focused lately.

"You don't look as chipper as you did last night," she says. "Are you sick? Why are you wearing a blanket?"

"Just cold. I'm still getting used to the climate."

"Hmm." She scowls. "It's at least a hundred degrees here."

"It's okay. Tell me why you quit your job."

"Quit might not be the right word exactly."

"Lilah. What's the right word?"

"Fired?"

"Oh my God. Lilah. What did you do?"

"I might have tossed a glass of beer into someone's face."

"Did he deserve it?"

"She. She definitely deserved it."

"What did she do?" I pull my feet up under me on the couch and adjust the blanket around my shoulders.

"It doesn't matter." She blows her shoulder length hair out of her eyes. "So I was thinking... maybe I could come up there. Visit you."

"And do some painting."

"Yes! But I don't want to interrupt your time alone."

I bite my lip to keep from laughing out loud. My time alone has been spent mostly with either Claire or Bradley. "Sure," I say. "I'd like you to come visit me."

Lilah's face brightens. "I was hoping you'd say that."

"You're already packed, aren't you?"

"How did you know?"

"Older sister super powers." Bradley would understand.

Speaking of Bradley, Lilah is going to need to know about the threat I got and not only that, she's going to need to know about Bradley and how he's staying here. To keep me safe.

"When are you leaving?" I ask.

She has the decency to look sheepish. "I just passed by your old exit."

"You're in Katy?"

"Yes. I hope that's okay."

She knew it was. She absolutely knew it was.

"And?"

She shrugs. How did I not notice she was driving?

"It's a little sister super power," she says, impishly.

"Right." And just for that, I'm going to make her wait to tell her what's going on up here.

My biggest concern is going to be keeping her out of trouble. After what happened to Claire, I'm going to have to convince her not to go anywhere alone, especially after dark.

It shouldn't be too much trouble. As long as she has paints and cavasses, she's good. Brianna might be a different story completely. Brianna does not like to stay home alone.

"Did you brings paints and supplies?"

"Of course. I might have forgotten my pajamas, though."

"That just so does not surprise me. Okay. Drive safely. And text me every time you stop."

"Yes, Mother. I'll do it." But she doesn't look the least bit put out.

This is an adventure for her just as it was for me.

She'll be here in a couple of days. I have to get her room ready. Wash the sheets. Clean and stock the bathroom.

I'm excited to see my sister and yet... I'm not ready to share my time with Bradley.

That's just irrational.

I sit for a minute. Thinking.

I have to tell Lilah what's happening. If for no other reason than for her own safety.

FORTY-SEVEN

Bradley

"ARE you headed back over to the widow's house?" Wyatt asks as we tool up after putting in several hours of work at the Bentley place.

"Audrey. Her name is Audrey."

"Okay. Are you headed back over to Audrey's house?"

"Yes. We still don't know who left threats on the front porch."

"That's a bit disturbing. Did the sheriff say anything?"

"You know he didn't. Might as well keep him out of the loop on something like this."

"You should run for sheriff."

"Not a chance. If any of us were going to run for sheriff, it would be Caleb."

"Caleb could do it."

"I don't know why he would want to."

"I don't either."

I look over at Wyatt. "You brought it up. Why don't you do it?"

"It's not really my thing."

"Something going on with you?" I open the door for Biscuit to hop inside the truck.

"I just think you'd make a good sheriff. I know you don't want to do it. My two cents. Take it or leave it." Wyatt kicks his back tire and, satisfied with it, opens the driver's door of his truck.

"Thanks for the vote of confidence. But I'd just as soon leave it."

"Audrey's sister coming up yet?"

"She has two of them. And you'll be the first to know."

"Sounds good."

"What's with you and Audrey's sisters?"

Wyatt laughs. "You're so easy to stir up. Have fun. And watch your back."

"You too."

I close the truck door and start up the motor.

Wyatt knows he can mess with me because he can tell I like Audrey.

Just as I'm about to pull out onto the road behind Wyatt, my phone rings.

It's the sheriff.

"Claire woke up," he blurts out in lieu of a greeting.

"Okay. That's good. How is she?" And more importantly has she said anything?

"She hasn't said anything yet."

"But she's conscious?"

"That's what they're saying. I haven't been down there." He takes a breath and I have a feeling I know the real reason he's calling. Sometimes I hate it when I'm right. "She doesn't have any family. Maybe you and Audrey should drive down there to see her?"

"To Boulder?"

"That's where they took her."

Damn it. Visiting Claire was not in my plans.

"I don't want to bother her. I'm thinking it's best to just wait until she gets home."

"Alright. I'm sure they'll figure out a way to get her home."

I'm not biting on that one. "I'm sure they will. I'll give Audrey the update."

I disconnect the line and head toward town.

On a whim, I stop by the pizza parlor and order a pizza to go.

I enjoy cooking with Audrey, but she and I should probably get some work done. Maybe change out her door locks, if the new ones came in, or measure for her window shades, or start floating sheetrock in her closet. She's got to be tired of living out of suitcases.

And then I have some bathroom renovations to bring up. She seems open to modernizing things, but we've got to actually get something finished at some point.

As I sit waiting for the pizza, I replay my conversation with the sheriff. How did he know that I was hanging out with Audrey?

I'd taken those flowers into his office, but I'd done that as a neighbor.

He's making the assumption that there's more to my relationship with her.

How could he possibly know?

How could he possibly know... and be right?

CHAPTER
FORTY-EIGHT

Audrey

I'm sitting in front of the fireplace, researching random career options when I hear Bradley's truck driving up.

I'd told Brianna that working is important for me. The problem is I don't really have a career. I have a degree in business, but working in business never really interested me. Kind of wish I'd realized that before I graduated. Still. Having the degree had gotten me the couple of jobs I'd had.

My fire is much bigger than I know is recommended, and just as he mentioned in a roundabout way, I'm going to run out of firewood sooner rather than later.

I close my iPad and get up, stretching.

I'd actually expected Bradley a couple of hours ago despite telling myself how irrational that expectation is.

Bradley doesn't actually live here. Bradley and I are not in a relationship.

He's just staying here until we find out who threatened me.

Then, once that's settled, he'll be on his way.

In the meantime, I get to live in a make believe world where Bradley lives here with me.

Meeting him at the door, I'm delighted to see that he brought pizza.

"Hello Biscuit." I rub the dog's head and he prances like an excited puppy.

"You brought pizza," I say, taking the box from Bradley.

"I was thinking we could work on something tonight."

"Sure. What do you want to work on?"

"Your wish is my command."

"That's a rather dangerous thing to say to a girl."

"What can I say? I live on the edge."

"You do, don't you? Did you say you're on the volunteer fire department?"

"I don't remember saying. But I am. They know they can call me whenever they need me. For whatever they need me for."

I wonder why they didn't call him the night Claire disappeared. But I don't ask.

"Speaking of," he says. "Claire woke up."

"What? Really? Did she say anything?"

"Not that I know of. She doesn't have any family."

"Oh. She has that guy who pays her. Mr. Fields? Did you find out who he is?"

"I didn't think to ask anyone yet. I was kind of giving Claire time to recover."

"Right." I take the pizza into the kitchen and open up the box.

"It's still hot," I say. "Want to eat while it's hot?"

"Sure."

I take down two plates and put two slices of pizza on each. Then on second thought, I add a third slice to Bradley's place and take them with me over to the fireplace.

"Want a beer?" I ask.

"Not right now. There might be power tools later."

"Right."

"Nice fire."

"I know. It's not your elegant fire. But the house was dreary."

"You're going to love winter."

"I'm getting the idea that you're being facetious about that."

"I might be."

The pizza has lots of gooey cheese. Just the way I like it.

I read the message that pops up on my phone. "My sister, Lilah."

"Is she okay?"

"Yes." I look into his eyes and in that moment I really wish I'd found a way to tell Lilah no. That it's not a good time for her to visit. "She's stopping for the night."

He looks at me sideways. "Stopping as in driving?"

"Yes. She's on her way here."

"Oh." He's quite good at hiding his surprise about this and I don't see any disappointment. So now I feel silly worrying about her interrupted our time together. "That's unexpected, isn't it?"

"Quite. There was some kind of problem with her job. She's been thinking about quitting anyway."

"Are you happy about it?" he asks.

"It'll be good to see her," I say, evading the question.

"Wyatt will be happy," he murmurs.

"Wyatt? Why?"

"Nothing. We should probably get to work on her room then."

"That's what I was thinking."

FORTY-NINE

Bradley

AFTER I SHOW Audrey how to apply the mesh tape, she proves to be an exceptional assistant. We get her closet taped up in no time.

"So what do you think?" I ask as I gather up the supplies to mix the powdered compound.

"About what?"

"Becoming a handyman's assistant?"

She gives me a sideways look. "Depends on the handyman."

"That's an interesting answer." I give her a grin as I

turn on the faucet to fill the plastic bucket. And one that I happen to like.

"Are you making me a job offer?" she asks, keeping her tone light, but not looking at me.

I turn off the water and sit on the edge of the bathtub.

"That depends. Are you available?"

She looks over at me, meeting my gaze now. "I'll consider it."

And then there's a sound. Faint. A soft creak from downstairs. Like a door easing open.

The wind?

Or something else?

We both freeze. Her eyes widen, not leaving mine.

Biscuit sits up from where he had been sleeping on the bathroom floor. A low grumble echoes from his throat.

"Stay here," I say, much calmer than I feel. "I'll go see what it was."

"I'm coming with you."

Biscuit stands up and darts out of the bathroom at a run.

"I guess we're all going," I say. "Stay behind me."

"Not a problem."

We leave the bathroom and start quietly down the hallway toward the stairs.

"Why is Biscuit being so quiet?"

"I don't know." But I do know that if someone hurts my dog, there will be serious hell to pay.

At the top of the stairs, we find Biscuit sitting quietly in front of the closed door.

I glance back at Audrey who looks as confused as I feel.

By the time we reach the bottom of the stairs, I'm regretting not setting her up with window shades already.

I hadn't realized it was already dark, but the windows with such lovely views during the day are no more than walls of darkness.

We can't see out, but others can easily see in.

With Audrey at my heels, I walk across to the door and put a hand on Biscuit's head. He shifts, standing, then sits back down.

I look out one window and Audrey looks out the one on the other side of the door.

"See anything?" I whisper.

"Nothing."

"Biscuit. Stay. I'm going out there to look."

Audrey holds Biscuit's collar, even though I don't think she can hold him unless he chooses to let her. He's much too strong and big.

I flip on the porch light and crack the door. Nothing there but the wind blowing lightly in the trees.

The porch creaks under my foot as I step out. The wind brushes against my face, cool and dry, and I scan the yard. Shadows dance across the grass. Just branches shifting, I think. Hope. I descend the steps slowly, listening.

Nothing moves.

No footsteps.

No voices.

Just the wind.

I take another step forward—and that's when I see it.

A small object rests on the edge of the porch. Something that wasn't there before.

I crouch down, heart thudding, and pick it up. A plain, cream-colored envelope. No name on the front. No stamp. The flap tucked closed, not sealed. I hesitate, then pull it open and slide out a single folded sheet of paper.

You were warned, Audrey.
Go now, while you can.

No signature. No explanation.

Behind me, I hear the door creak open. Audrey's voice is quiet. "What is it?"

I fold the note and tuck it into my pocket. "Nothing. Just trash. Probably blew in with the wind."

She steps onto the porch, barefoot. Her eyes search mine.

I hold her gaze, but I don't say more.

Not yet.

Because I don't know who left the note.

I don't know what *while you can* means.

But I do know one thing. Someone doesn't want her here.

And that turns the worry in my gut into something sharper. Something burning.

Anger.

She deserves to know the truth.

And I won't keep her in the dark.

Not when shadows are starting to gather.

"Let's go inside."

CHAPTER
FIFTY

Audrey

BRADLEY and I sit together in front of the fireplace, turned toward each other. Biscuit takes his place in front of the fireplace.

"We need to talk about this," Bradley says.

"About what?" I search his eyes, but I don't like what I see there.

Anger.

Even though I know it's not directed toward me, I feel the heat of it.

"These threats."

"What was out there?" I ask. "You said it was just trash blowing up."

With a sigh, he reaches into his pocket and pulls out an envelope.

"I can't not tell you," he says, putting the note in my hand.

"Another one?"

"Yeah. This one looks more rushed. Less planned."

"It's just an envelope," I muse. "No elaborate presentation like the one in the black box."

I pull the letter out of the envelope.

You were warned, Audrey.
Go now, while you can.

"I GUESS we at least know who the threat is directed toward," I say, putting the note back in his hand.

"This has to stop. I'm going to make it stop."

"How?"

"I don't know yet. but it's gone too far."

"What are you going to do? Chase the wind?"

"Somebody wants us to find these notes. They're going to a lot of trouble to do it. And risk. Somebody is coming up here, risking us seeing them leave these notes."

"I know, but…"

"Security cameras. I'm driving into Boulder tomorrow and getting some cameras. We're going to have security cameras all over this place."

"That might work."

"It will," he says with determination and certainty. "We'll find out who's doing this and I'll put a stop to it."

"Okay." I take a deep, shuddering breath. "Okay. We'll put a stop to it."

"You still don't think we need to tell the sheriff?"

"I don't think it'll do any good."

"I haven't told Lilah what she's walking into yet."

"Hopefully we'll get it sorted out before much longer. But…" he looks into my eyes. "when she gets here, you have to tell her."

"I know."

"You have to tell her so she can watch for anything unusual. And I don't think either one of you need to go anywhere alone. Not until after we at least talk to Claire."

"When is that going to happen?"

"I wasn't going to do it, but tomorrow when I'm in Boulder getting security cameras, I'll stop in and see if she remembers anything."

"Okay. Do you want me to go with you?"

"You can if you want to. But… when is Lilah getting here?"

I glance at my phone. "Not sure. Possibly tomorrow."

"I'll leave Biscuit here with you tomorrow."

"Really? That sounds like a great idea."

"Now," he says. "We've got some walls to mud."

"Sounds like fun," I say.

"You have no idea."

He gets up. Holds out a hand. "Let's go do something fun."

Putting my hand in his, I get to my feet.

Anything I do with Bradley is fun.

Sitting in front of the fireplace. Cooking. Taping walls with mesh tape.

Even... almost... chasing the wind.

FIFTY-ONE

Bradley

I'D HARDLY LEFT Audrey's house and made it past my own before I was regretting leaving not only Biscuit, but also Audrey behind.

I came so close to stopping and turning around that I slowed to a crawl for a few minutes.

But Audrey wasn't up yet, first of all, and second, I want to get to Boulder and get back as soon as possible.

I want to get those security cameras and get them installed. Enough is enough.

And I need to talk to Claire. By going to the hospital

where she is, I'm running the risk of having to drive her back to Whiskey Springs. But if I do, then I just do.

If I can find out why she was unconscious on the side of the road, any inconvenience will be worth it.

As a compromise to myself, I call Wyatt and wake him up. Tell him what I'm doing.

"See," he says. "You'd be a good sheriff. Nobody else though about putting cameras up around the house and it's such a simple thing. I should have thought of it. The sheriff should have thought about it."

"I guess we were all hoping there was nothing to it. That it would blow over."

"Doesn't look like that's happening. Do you want me to ride down with you?"

"Actually, Audrey has strict instructions to call me if anything feels off. I left Biscuit with her—"

"You left Biscuit. Dude. I think you have it bad."

"No comment. But if she calls me, I'm going to need you on standby."

"Got it. I can do that. Just let me know. Been a while since I've gotten the chance to kick someone's ass."

"Well." I pull out onto the highway. "That sounds like a story to be heard over a beer."

"You might be right."

"Oh. And guess what? You'll be happy to know that her sister, Lilah is on her way up here."

"Get out."

"No. I'm serious. So it's possible you'll get to meet her."

"I hope you know I was funning with you."

"Well, I'm not funning. She really is on the way here."

"Huh."

"And now I see the cat's got your tongue."

"I'll probably meet her on my next firewood delivery."

"Probably."

"I still think you should run for sheriff."

"Don't change the subject."

"Okay. Well. Since I'm on standby, I might as well get up and make myself a cup of coffee."

"I'll call you when I get back. We'll install cameras."

"I'll be ready."

My drive into Boulder is uneventful. Boulder, however, is a busy little city. Almost too much traffic for their infrastructure. Just an observation. Not my bailiwick. Although, I'm beginning to think maybe I should have considered civil engineering. I seem to notice things that a civil engineer would notice.

I did some Internet searching last night, so I know right where to go to get the best cameras at the best deal. While I'm there at the hardwood store, I get Audrey a new fireplace poker set. It's halfway supposed to be a joke that makes her smile, but mostly something she really needs.

I noticed that hers is getting worn out. I've had to screw the handle back on twice.

After that, I do a couple more errands, then head to the hospital to see if I can talk to Claire.

Unfortunately the staff denies that she's there.

Back in my truck, I give the sheriff a call.

"I tried to see Claire. They told me she's not there."

"She's there. She must have opted out of visitors."

"Then maybe as sheriff, you should drive down here and talk to her yourself instead of sending someone else."

"Maybe I will."

"I meant to ask you if you know someone named Mr. Fields that Claire might work for."

"I don't, but I'll see what I can find out."

"Thanks. By the way, Audrey has gotten two threatening notes left on her doorstep."

"You're just now telling me this?"

"You didn't seem all that interested when I brought those flowers in for you to check on."

"Those were flowers. Not threatening notes. I'll drive up there and take a look around."

"Sounds good. Audrey's there by herself today."

"I'll go by there. Take a look."

"Thanks. I'm about to lose service. Later."

Damn it. I hate it when Wyatt puts stuff in my head. I would be a good sheriff. But I'm an engineer. A handyman. Not a lawman.

Traffic is bad through the canyon. Everybody thinks they have to drive around the sharp curves like they're driving on a race track.

Makes me appreciate the small town of Whiskey Springs all the more.

If not for getting the cameras, I would have called it a wasted trip. The cameras, however, make it worthwhile. Faster than ordering and waiting on a delivery.

Wyatt has experience in installing cameras like this, so I'm really surprised he didn't think of it before I did.

At any rate, I'm going to put him to work helping me install them. They'll be up and running long before nightfall. Time to put an end to the nonsense.

FIFTY-TWO

Audrey

I'M IN MY BEDROOM, sketching out some possible designs for my closet, when I hear a vehicle coming down my road.

It doesn't sound like Bradley's truck and it isn't the mailman.

I go to the window and look out.

It's a police car. My heart slams in my chest.

My first thought is that something is wrong.

I flash back to the police officer that had come to my house after Thomas's accident. It hadn't mattered that the FAA had already called me. The officer coming by my house had been the final confirmation that my world had shattered.

But this isn't that.

No one would know how to get in touch with me here.

I reflexively glance at my phone. No calls or messages.

Taking a deep breath, I wait for the buzzing in my ears to quiet.

Instead of going downstairs, I stand at the window and watch the sheriff get out of his car. He doesn't come to the door, though. Instead, he walks around, looking.

When the officer's car door slams shut, Biscuit, who had been sleeping on the foot of my bed, jumps down from the bed and with a low growl in his throat, shoots out of the bedroom and gallops down the stairs.

The officer isn't very old. Thirties maybe. Tall and clean-shaven from what I can see from here.

Surely he knows I'm home. My car is parked next to the house. Hard to miss.

Maybe Bradley told him about the notes.

I call Bradley's number, but it goes straight to voicemail.

Well. I tried.

When the officer turns and sees me standing in the window, I sigh. There's no getting away from facing whatever this is.

I follow Biscuit downstairs and put a hand on his collar while I crack the door open.

"Audrey Sinclair?" the officer asks.

"Yes." I keep one hand on the doorknob and the other on Biscuit's collar. My heart is still beating too fast.

"I'm Sheriff Morgan. Hey Biscuit."

Biscuit barks once, obviously recognizing the sheriff. That alleviates a little of my anxiety.

Sheriff Morgan is a large man. Tall and stocky with an imposing frown on his features. He fills the doorway and is not a little intimidating. It doesn't help that he's wearing reflective sun glasses, hiding his eyes from me.

"How can I help you?"

"I heard you've been having some trouble around here."

"Right." Another layer of anxiety drops off. He's not here to tell me anything. He's here because of the threats. "Did Bradley talk to you?"

He drags off his sun glasses, making him look a little bit less intimidating. There's a kindness in his eyes that I hadn't been able to see behind the sun glasses. "Something about some notes?"

"Yes. Do you want to see them?"

"Might be helpful." Although his words are sarcastic, he sounds genuine.

I step back to let him inside. As the door widens, Biscuit bolts outside, jerking free of my hand.

"Biscuit!" I call out for him, but he's headed toward the trees.

I glance helplessly from the dog to the sheriff. We don't usually let Biscuit go out front. He should be okay and I don't think he'll run off, but if anything happens to Bradley's dog on my watch…I don't even want to think about it.

"The notes are on the kitchen island."

"Go," he says. "I'll take a look at them."

"Okay. Thank you." Leaving the sheriff, I rush down the porch steps toward Biscuit.

I realize I must have forgotten to take him out for a walk because he's already digging a hole in the dirt.

By the time Biscuit and I are heading back toward the door, the sheriff is coming out the front door.

"Did you find them?" I ask, referring to the threatening letters.

"Yes." He taps his shirt pocket. "I'm just going to take them with me. Start an investigation."

"Okay," I say. "If that's what you need to do."

"It's the only way to find out who's doing it."

Biscuit rubs the sheriff's hand. Patting Biscuit on the head, the sheriff smiles at me. Somehow seeing him smile doesn't comfort me any. In fact, his smile seems forced, unnatural even. But I just met the sheriff, for all of half a second ago, so I'm in no place to judge him one way or another.

As I stand at the window, watching him drive off, I breathe a sigh of relief.

I can't explain it, but him showing up like this unannounced without Bradley here leaves me feeling unsettled.

FIFTY-THREE

Bradley

"HAND ME THAT DRILL," Wyatt says, from his perch on a ladder balanced against one of the blue spruce trees out behind Audrey's house.

"You sure we have to put these cameras up here in the trees?" I ask, glancing around before putting my attention back on the iPad in my hands.

Wyatt glances down at me. "Would you rather people just see them when they drive up?"

"Good point. I should have gotten the camouflage ones."

"These are good quality. You did good."

"Turn it a little bit to the left."

Wyatt turns the camera.

"Good. Better."

"Let me see."

I pass the iPad up to Wyatt. He makes some minor adjustments to the camera position and hands the iPad back.

"You're really good at this," I say.

"It's why I get paid the big bucks."

"Too bad there aren't very many people in Whiskey Springs who need security cameras installed."

"More than you'd think, but I can't charge people like Audrey. I have to go into Boulder and other places outside of town to actually charge people a premium price."

"You should get with Caleb. Let him set up the business side of it for you. Do some advertisements."

"Nah. Word of mouth gets me plenty of work."

"Still. Caleb could set you up a price structure."

Wyatt climbs down the ladder. "You do realize Caleb has nothing on me, right?"

"Actually. No. I always think of Caleb as being the business brains out of the three of us."

"If Caleb's the business brains, what am I?"

"Same as me. The worker. But you're good with electronics and oddly enough, forestry. I'm better with renovations."

"I guess we all have our strengths."

"Where do you think the next one needs to go?"

"Need to cover that blind spot over on the side of the house."

"Have to attach it to the external wall."

"It won't be noticeable."

Audrey comes out the back door.

"How's it going?" she asks.

"Take a look so far," I say, showing her the iPad.

"That's rather impressive. I think we're about to break this game up. So I heard from Lilah. She stopped for the night, but she'll be here in the morning."

"Good. That gives us time to get these security cameras up. I'll feel a whole lot better once all this is in place."

"Me too."

"Wyatt. I've got cold beer in the fridge when you get through."

"You didn't offer me a beer," I tell her.

"Didn't know I had to." She turns and walks back inside.

Wyatt props the ladder against the side of the house. "She's sweet on you."

"Just showing her appreciation."

"Whatever you want to tell yourself."

"She's still grieving."

"Been what? Four weeks?"

"Hardly time to get past the initial shock," I say.

"Maybe." He climbs up the ladder. "Hand me one of those cameras."

I hand one of the cameras up to him.

"Everybody is different," he says. "There's no clock to punch on things like that."

"When did you get to be so smart?"

"Always being underestimated."

"The youngest son always has such a hard life."

"You have no idea."

"Tomorrow you get to meet Lilah."

"Tomorrow I will be working over at the Danbury cabin."

"What's wrong with the Danbury cabin?"

"Got to replace a dishwasher."

"You're just trying to avoid meeting the sister."

"I told you I was just funning."

"Chicken."

"Maybe. Let me see that iPad."

I hand the iPad up to him.

It's nice. Spending time like this with my brother. Getting to see him do what he does best. Flipping our roles so that I'm the helper and he's the expert.

"One more camera to install. Then I'm going to have that beer. Then I'm going to head out. Let you have some time with Audrey before her sister gets here."

"I keep telling you, it's not like that."

Wyatt looks down at me. "Then maybe it should be like that. Nothing changes if nothing changes."

I hate it when Wyatt is right.

"You think any more about running for sheriff?" he asks, back on the ground.

"Good God, Wyatt. How many times do I have to tell you? I'm not interested in running for sheriff."

FIFTY-FOUR

Audrey

SITTING on the sofa in front of what everyone calls my too big fire in the fireplace with Bradley and Wyatt reminds me of hanging out with my two sisters.

The two brothers tease each other mercilessly while supporting each other with no qualms whatsoever.

I sit with my iPad in my lap, watching the six cameras all on the screen at once. It's a good app. I can touch any one of the six camera to zoom in. Then just slide it back into place so I can see all six again. And they are all recording constantly.

Nobody is going to be sneaking up on us leaving

threatening notes on the porch or anywhere else without being caught on camera.

"I'm heading out," Wyatt says. "Got an early day tomorrow."

"Thanks Wyatt," I say. "For installing the cameras. I can't tell you how much better I feel having them up."

"Bradley drove into the city and bought them. I just installed them."

"Then thanks to both of you."

"I'll walk you to the door," Bradley says.

Using my iPad, I watch them standing out on the porch, zooming in just to get used to handling the app. I don't have the volume turned on, so I don't know what they're saying. I don't want to know.

I do however study the two men. Both are handsome and they look like brothers even though Wyatt is more rugged looking.

Bradley, in my opinion is the handsome one. It baffles me how no one has scooped him up already. As far as I can tell neither one of them has a girlfriend, at least not right now.

I'm about as close to an unofficial girlfriend as Bradley can get. It would be hard for him to have a girlfriend while spending his nights over here with me.

Bradley comes back in and I use the camera to watch Wyatt get in his truck and leave the driveway.

"Wyatt ordered some cameras to put down the road

so we can see anyone driving up. He'll come back and install those when they come in."

"He's a good guy."

"Of course."

"I need to pay him for doing all this work."

"You'll do nothing of the sort. He did it as a favor to me. If you go offering him money, he'll be insulted."

"How could anyone be insulted by taking money for work for hire?"

"A favor," he says. "What can I make you for dinner?"

"I could just eat a salad."

"I don't see how you do it."

"What's that?" I join him in the kitchen, setting the iPad on the island so we can watch it while we make dinner.

"Have the willpower to eat healthy like you do."

"It's not easy. Not when you cook such good pasta."

"You like my pasta?" I grin, ridiculously pleased.

"LOVE your pasta."

"I think there's still some left over if you'd like it."

"Okay.

"Okay then. Pasta it is."

I smile and our gazes lock.

There is something so very comfortable about spending a simple evening at home with Bradley.

I don't know what to make of him. He's never tried to kiss me. I don't know if he even likes me romantically.

Taking a wooden bowl from the cabinet to make a salad, I admonish myself.

I shouldn't be thinking about Bradley like this.

As a newly widowed woman, it's not appropriate. I should *not* be thinking about him romantically.

Setting a pot of water to boil for noodles, he smiles over at me and my heart flutters like a teenager.

Just because I *shouldn't* be thinking about kissing him, does not mean I'm not thinking about it.

What girl wouldn't be thinking about kissing Bradley? Certainly not any girl he looks at with that twinkle in his eyes.

I'm hopeless. Just hopelessly hopeless when it comes to Bradley Winslow.

I'm not sure I'd change that particular truth even if I could.

CHAPTER
FIFTY-FIVE

Bradley

AFTER DINNER, I sit on the edge of the hearth assembling the poker set I bought Audrey.

"You thought it was time to retire my fireplace tools?" she asks, glancing up from her iPad. She's been watching the camera images all evening.

"They were worn out when you got here."

"I know. I didn't do it. Still. It was kind of you to replace them. Thank you."

My phone chimes with a text message.

I lean over to where I'd left it on the sofa and look at it.

"Everything okay?" Audrey asks, seeing my expression.

"It's my dad. Claire is coming home tomorrow."

"How does your dad know this?"

"I have no idea." I set the phone down and go back to tending the fire. "Small town? Everybody knows everything about everybody."

She wrinkles her nose. "Does that mean we're going to see her tomorrow?"

I like the way she just tosses out that word *we* like it's the most natural thing in the world.

"I think so. I really want to know what happened."

Audrey looks up from her iPad. "I hope she can tell us."

"What do you mean?"

"She was unconscious. She might not know."

"She'll know." I have to believe that. I have to believe that we can at least find out if she had anything to do with the threatening letters.

"Claire didn't do it," Audrey says suddenly, looking at me.

"How do you know?"

"Because she was in the hospital when the second note was left."

"You're right. You're absolutely right."

"We still need to know what happened. If the same person that left the note tried to hurt her."

"We'll find out." I turn back around to poke at the fire

some more. It's soothing, messing with the logs and watching the flames.

Audrey makes a sound that has me looking over my shoulder at her. "See something?"

She shakes her head. "I thought I did, but it's just the wind."

"You know those are recording, right?"

"I know."

I get up and go to sit next to her. Hold out a hand for the iPad. "How about we take a break from the surveillance?"

"Okay." She hands me the iPad and watches as I close the cover and set it aside.

I turn toward her. Take her hands in mine.

"It's going to be okay," I say. "We've got a good start to measuring the windows. We'll finish that up tomorrow and get some window shades ordered. I think we'll both feel better when we have the windows covered."

"I've started looking. I still haven't decided what kind to order. Lilah will be here tomorrow. She's good at that kind of thing."

"Good. We both have siblings that are good at different things."

"Thank you," she says. "For being here."

"You don't have to thank me. I'm in it now."

"You didn't know what you were getting in to."

I squeeze her hands. "It wouldn't have mattered. I'd do it all over again."

"You're a good man. Why don't you have a girlfriend?"

"Maybe I'm working on that."

"Is that so? How are you working on that when you're here all the time?"

"Two birds with one stone."

Biscuit lifts his head and his ears tilt forward.

I let go of Audrey's hands and pick up the iPad to check the app.

"See anything?" she asks, leaning close enough to see.

"Just shadows."

Biscuit puts his head back down.

"Must have been a false alarm."

"Must have." I'm not ready to lose my excuse for staying here, but I am ready to find out who's leaving threatening notes. And whoever's doing it is bold enough to do it with my truck sitting outside. Knowing that I'm here and Audrey's not alone.

That in itself is disconcerting.

She yawns.

"You're tired," I say. "I'll walk you up to your room."

"You just got the fire going. Seems a shame to waste it."

"Biscuit is enjoying it."

"Yes he is."

"Come on," I say, standing up. I pull her up. "I'll monitor the iPad and you take your book." I pick up the novel she left on the coffee table and hand it to her.

"Maybe we'll get a reprieve tonight."

"Maybe."

"Bradley?"

"Yes?" On impulse, I take her hand and lead her toward the stairs.

"What if he... or she... knows about the cameras and doesn't bring any more notes?"

"Then I guess we solved the problem."

"I wish I had your optimism."

"I just refuse to live in fear."

She doesn't say anything.

I can't even begin to imagine what she's been through this last month or so.

The fact that she's even here. Functioning. Says a lot about her level of strength.

Just one more thing I like about her.

Audrey is an incredibly strong woman.

We reach the top of the stairs and stop at her bedroom door.

"Wake me up if anything happens on the cameras," she says.

"Okay." Even though I agree, I don't plan on waking her. She's practically asleep on her feet even now. If she can sleep, she needs to sleep.

I kiss her on the forehead. "Get some rest. I'll be here in the morning when you get up."

"No work tomorrow?"

"I want to catch up on some things here."

"Okay," she says, walking into her bedroom, leaving the door open.

"Do you want this closed?" I ask.

"No. You can leave it open."

"Okay." As she heads into her bathroom, I continue down the hall to my room.

Even the possibility of someone leaving threatening notes isn't enough to dampen my optimism right now. Things are looking up.

FIFTY-SIX

Audrey

AFTER GETTING READY, I climb into my bed and with the lamp on, open up my book to read a page or two.

Before I can open the book, though, I get a text from Lilah.

LILAH

I'll should be there early in the morning.

How early is early?

LILAH

Depends on what time I wake up. I'm two hours away.

> Okay. Let me know when you
> leave so I can be up.

LILAH

Good night.

I put my phone on charge and hold my book in my lap.

Instead of reading, though, I let myself replay my evening, specifically the way Bradley had kissed me on the forehead.

Definitely a show of affection. But maybe it was the way a brother would kiss a sister.

Not having any brothers, I don't really know.

It meant something, though, for me.

I'm letting myself get attached. No two ways about it. Not smart.

As soon as we catch the person leaving the threatening notes, Bradley will be leaving me here alone. As he should.

He's been such a perfect gentleman.

But I'm sure he has a life of his own. Maybe there's someone he wants to date. He's put his life on hold for me, a stranger in need.

I have to keep myself together. To remember that I came here for a couple of reasons. One because the house and money had been left to me. And second, to give myself the time and space to become accustomed to being a widow.

To figure out what it is I want to do next with my life. I've been too busy today to even think about finding a job.

And now Lilah is coming for a visit. Things will get even busier. It would be rude of me to start a new job while she's here visiting.

The job thing will just have to wait.

With a sigh, I open up my book to the place I have bookmarked.

But there along with my bookmark is a note.

With a chill running down my spine, I toss the book, my bookmark, and the note away from me.

My heart is pounding so fast, I put a hand over my chest. Take deep calming breaths.

I call out to Bradley, but his name gets stuck in my throat.

I hadn't opened the book since last night.

Someone had found a way to leave a note in it. Bypassed the security cameras.

I slide off the bed, sliding my feet into my slippers, then pick up the note with two fingers.

My heart pounding in my throat, I walk down the hall toward Bradley's room, holding the letter at arm's length.

His door is wide open. I hadn't expected that, but I don't have time to process it.

The second he sees me, he's out of bed and across the room.

He's wearing a pair of sleep pants and a white t-shirt.

"Where did you get that?" he asks.

I try to speak, but I can't get the words out. "I…"

He takes the note with one hand and grabs my hand with his other.

Leads me over to sit on the edge of the bed.

"Did you read it?" he asks. I shake my head. "No. You didn't read it."

He unfolds the letter and reads it silently.

"What does it say?"

"It's typed this time. It says *Don't think Bradley can protect you. Put up as many cameras as you want. You'll be leaving soon. One way or another.*"

"Let me see," I say, holding out my hand for the note. Surely I misunderstood him.

He hands me the note and stands up while I read it. Running a hand through his hair, he paces to the door and back. "This is too much. That's a bold threat."

"It's clearly a threat," I say, still staring at the paper. "How did it get in my book?"

"Someone was in the house again. Just like the flowers. Someone has a key."

I try to think. Had I left the house open today at any point? Only when Wyatt and Bradley had been outside mounting security cameras. Obviously a waste of time. But I'd been inside the house the whole time or just outside on the porch. No one could have gotten past me.

"What do we do?" I ask.

"I don't know." He comes back and sits next to me on the bed.

"We have to do something."

"We'll think of something." He takes the note. Sets it aside. "Are you okay?"

"I don't know. I will be." I don't have a choice. "I'll go back to bed now." Even though I know there's no way I'm going to be able to sleep. Not now.

He doesn't say anything and I don't make any moves to get up.

I'm still trembling.

"You don't have to go," he says. "Just stay here until you've had a chance to calm down."

"Okay." But I don't know if I'll ever calm down. Not completely. Not now.

You'll be leaving soon. One way or another.

Don't think Bradley can protect you. Put up as many cameras as you want.

It's like the person who did this has a direct line into my life. It's like they know everything.

They know about Bradley. About the cameras.

And they want me away from here.

One way or another.

I shiver a little as I consider just what that means. Dead or alive. That's what it means.

Whoever is doing this will do whatever it takes to run me out of this house.

"Maybe I should just go," I say. "Back to Houston."

"No," Bradley says, firmly. "We won't let this person run you away. You're tougher than that."

"I don't know. This feels bigger."

"Audrey," he says, putting a hand lightly beneath my chin.

I lift my gaze and look into his light blue eyes.

"I'm going to keep you safe, okay?"

I nod. "I know."

"Come here." He wraps me in his arms, holding me close against him. Resting my cheek against his chest, I listen to his steady heartbeat.

He holds me like I matter. Like I'm not just someone he promised to protect, but someone he never wants to let go of.

My fingers curl in the fabric of his shirt before I realize I've moved them, and I feel the breath he takes. Deep and deliberate. Before his chin brushes the top of my head. The scent of him is warm cedar and something darker, like coffee and days spent outside. It lingers in the air between us, stealing any thought of pulling away.

Outside, the wind rustles through the trees. Inside, it's just the two of us and this moment I'm not sure either of us knows how to define, much less name.

I haven't been this close to a man since Thomas. That thought lands like a stone in my chest. Unexpected and heavier than I want it to be. I thought my heart was done with this, that it had curled in on itself for good. But here I am, breathing this man in, and some long-quiet part of me is waking.

He doesn't loosen his hold, and I don't want him to. Because if I tilt my head back right now, I'm afraid we might close the rest of the space between us.

And I'm not sure I'd stop him.

His heartbeat stays steady, but mine... My heartbeat is doing its own uneven dance.He shifts just enough to look down at me, his gaze searching, his hand trailing from my shoulder to my elbow. Not a caress exactly, but it leaves a warm trail behind.

"You're trembling," he says quietly.

"I'm okay." My voice is steady enough, though I'm not sure if I'm trying to convince him or myself.

He studies me for a moment longer, then tucks a loose strand of hair behind my ear. The brush of his fingers along my cheek makes my breath catch.

"You don't have to be," he says. "Not with me."

For one dizzying second, I think he's going to kiss me. My pulse spikes, and every sensible thought is gone, replaced by the scent of him, the way his eyes have softened, the faint roughness of his jaw just inches from mine.

But then his arms loosen, and he leans back just enough that cool air rushes between us. The loss is almost physical.

"Come on," he says, voice low but different now, as if he's just as aware of what almost happened. "Let's get you tucked in for the night."

I nod, my throat too tight for words, and follow him out of his room down the hallway to my own. My body still remembers the heat of him, and my heart... well, it hasn't quite decided what to think or do yet.

FIFTY-SEVEN

Bradley

I'm TREADING on dangerous ground with Audrey.

Every cell in my body is urging me to kiss her. It would be so easy. No natural. So... right.

And yet I know it's not. It would be complicated. And messy. And so... wrong.

After she climbs into bed, I pull the blanket up over her shoulders, careful not to let my fingers linger. She's warm, soft, looking up at me with those tired, trusting eyes.

"Don't go," she whispers.

The words hit harder than they should. I'm not sure if

she means tonight... or in general. Either way, I feel them resonating in my chest.

I sit on the edge of the bed. "I'm not going anywhere."

Her hand finds mine in the dark, her fingers curling just enough to keep me there.

I stay. Listening to her breathing slow. Watching the way the clouds shift and the moonlight brushes over her face.

And trying, unsuccessfully, not to imagine what it would be like if I was allowed to be hers.

"Good night, sweetheart." Leaning over, I kiss her on the cheek. So soft and warm.

"Good night," she murmurs.

Leaving the door open, I make it as far as the hallway before I stop.

Every step away from her feels wrong, like I'm leaving something unfinished. The quiet in the house presses in on me, heavy and restless. Leaving her alone feels dangerous and wrong.

I turn back.

Her eyes are closed when I near the bed, but I know she's awake—the way her breathing changes, the tiniest shift of her shoulders.

I walk around to the other side of the large bed, the floorboards creaking under my weight.

I climb onto the bed, the mattress dipping, settle in beneath the blankets, and draw her back against me. She fits like she's always belonged there, her spine warm against my chest, her hair brushing my jaw.Every cell in my body urges me to lower my mouth to her shoulder, to close the last bit of space between us. It would be so easy. So natural. So... right.

And yet, my head is telling me not to cross that line. Not yet. It's too soon.

She's been through too much, too recently.

So I just hold her, my arm wrapped around her waist, my thumb tracing a slow, steady pattern against her hip beneath her cotton pajamas. Her breathing evens out, and I match mine to hers, letting the rhythm tether me to her.

Her soft hair against my cheek smells like jasmine. Her skin smells like honeysuckle.

I can tell when she relaxes and drifts asleep.

So soft against me. Her round behind pressed against me.

There's no going back from this.

Audrey is the woman I've been searching for my whole life.

If I have to wait for her. To wait until she's ready to go to the next level, then that's what I'll do. I'll wait. I'll wait an eternity for her if I have to.

She makes me feel whole. In a way I've never felt like before.

I hadn't realized until this moment that she's the one I've been waiting for.

I'm not sure if I'm keeping her safe tonight... or if she's the one keeping me.

CHAPTER
FIFTY-EIGHT

Audrey

I WAKE the next morning with sunlight across my face. I feel its warmth even before I open my eyes.

I don't even know what time it is. All I know is that I can't remember the last time I slept so soundly through the night.

Stretching beneath the sheets, I run a hand along the empty side of the bed and catch the scent of warm cedar and outdoors.

Bradley.

My mind flashes back to last night. To feeling safe and

warm. And I can't remember the last time I felt so content.

Bradley hadn't left me alone. I don't how long he stayed, but I remember him being here. Holding me.

Keeping me safe.

He hadn't had to do that, but he had.

I'd been frightened by the note I'd found tucked in the pages of my book like an ominous bookmark.

The words had left no doubt about the seriousness of the threat. Whoever wrote it knew everything. Knew about Bradley keeping me safe. And most importantly, knew about the cameras.

So it had been all for naught. Since the person making the threats knew about the cameras, we'd put them up for nothing.

Even more terrifying, he had bypassed our whole system and put a threatening note right here in my book. Right beneath our noses.

Heading into the bathroom, I start thinking about those heated floors again. And the gas fireplace in the bathroom.

Bradley might not appreciate me adding things to my list of things house renovations.

As I stand in the shower, the hot water streaming over my head, I remember that Lilah is coming today. She'd stopped for the night just two hours from here.

I never thought of Lila being particularly practical, but

waiting until morning to make the drive up into the mountains is just that. Smart and practical.

I'm quite impressed with her doing that. Had I mentioned how hard the drive was at night? I don't remember, but she probably did her research either way.

I decide on a pair of jeans and a comfortable sweatshirt for the day. I've learned that it doesn't matter that it's summer. It's still cold here in the mountains above Whiskey Springs.

Even when the sun comes out, the wind has a chill to it.

I don't envy the people living in Houston. Not even a little bit. I'll take the cold any day.

Dressed, I head out and hear Biscuit let out a bark before he runs in my direction. He meets me at the bottom of the stairs. Wriggling all over and licking me, he acts like he hasn't seen me for days.

I scratch his head and laugh at him. "What's gotten into you?" I ask the dog.

He just turns and runs toward the kitchen where Bradley is standing at the stove.

"Good morning," he says, tossing a towel over his shoulder.

"Hi. What's gotten into Biscuit?" the dog trails along at my feet.

"I don't know. Maybe he's just happy to see you."

"Maybe. What are you doing?"

"I'm making you breakfast."

"Oh." I sit down on the nearest bar stool.

"Is that okay?"

"It is. It's wonderful. It's just…" I watch him flip an omelet. "I don't know what I did to deserve so much kindness."

"I just want to make you happy," he says, coming around the kitchen island, leaning over, and kissing me on the forehead. "How did you sleep?"

"I can't remember the last time I slept so well."

"It's the clean mountain air," he says, going back to flipping the omelet.

I watch him a moment as I replay a memory of sleeping curled up against him.

"Yes," I say. "I'm sure that's it."

He grins. "So. Your sister will be here this morning." He makes a cup of coffee in the fancy machine and puts it in front of me.

"Yes." I glance out the window. The coffee is just the way I like it. "The roads should be clear, right?"

"I think so. Why don't I take off after breakfast? Give you time to get her settled?" He glances at the iPad open to the security camera app. "You're got the cameras and I have the app on my phone, too."

I swallow thickly, realizing I don't want him to go. Realizing I'd been expecting him to be here when Lilah got here.

I'd been looking forward to introducing them.

Looking forward to Bradley getting to know my family, starting with Lilah and for them to get to know him.

"Okay," I say. "Sure. What about Claire? Claire is coming home today, right? We were going to go talk to her."

"I'll go. You'll have Lilah here."

"Right. I don't want to drag her into this, especially not right away."

"I wouldn't think so."

"You don't have to go out of your way to go talk to her though."

He scoops up an omelet, puts half of it in on one plate and sets it in front of me. Puts the other half on another plate for himself and sits down next to me. "I want to go talk to her. I need to. I need to know what happened that night. There's too much coincidence. I'd like to be able to make sense of it."

"So would I. This looks wonderful." I take a bite. "It is wonderful."

"I'm glad you like it."

"You know," I say. "I'm not sure you realize what you're doing here."

"What am I doing?"

"You're going to make it hard for me to let you go."

He doesn't say anything. He just grins.

CHAPTER
FIFTY-NINE

Bradley

TRUE TO MY WORD, I clean up from making breakfast and head out.

Audrey and I didn't talk this morning about anything serious. She's focused on her sister's arrival. As she should be.

I left Biscuit with her again today. Not that I don't want to take him with me, but it's good for her to have him there. Biscuit is a good enough guard dog.

Relieved that the roads are clear, I drive past my house and keep going. I'll go by later and change out my clothes, but right now I have something I need to do.

Audrey and I didn't talk about the threatening note she found tucked in her book last night.

We didn't talk about sleeping with her curled in my arms.

And we didn't talk about how she'd actually laughed when she'd met Biscuit coming down the stairs. She hadn't even realized she was laughing. It had been spontaneous and real.

And it had warmed my heart.

She's healing.

And as she's healing, she and I are getting closer and closer.

She'd been onto something when she'd told me cooking for her would make it hard for her to let me go.

Maybe I hadn't done it consciously, but subconsciously, that was sort of the whole point.

I didn't want her to let me go.

She'd told me she couldn't move out of the house. That she has to live in the house in order for the inheritance to be valid.

I pull out onto the main highway and head toward Whiskey Springs.

So okay. I get that she wants to make sure she keeps the house.

I, on the other hand, have never lived anywhere that I found to be all that important. Probably the result of living in several of my family's cabins since I'd come back from Purdue.

It was convenient to live in a place while I was doing renovations there.

It had also made it easier for me let go of places. To see a house as just a place to live.

Some people think of their houses as an extension of themselves.

I think maybe my parents might be attached to their house. But I get that. They'd built it from the ground up right after they'd gotten married. It's their home. They had raised a family there. Three boys.

That's probably different. They have a lot of memories tied up there.

My brothers and I have a more transient mindset.

Long way around to say that if she wants to live in the Albright house, I have no problem living there with her. On the contrary. There are plenty of things she and I can do to make it better.

I'd planned on staying around today and doing some of those things, but then I'd remembered that her sister was coming in.

I don't want to make things complicated for her. For her to have to explain why I'm there.

I can only imagine that that would be awkward. Lilah expects to find her sister up here all alone, grieving for the sudden loss of a husband.

I can readily admit that I'd had something to do with that not happening quite so much.

Not my fault though. Not my fault that someone is

leaving Audrey threatening notes. If that someone, if anyone, so much as touches a hair on Audrey's head, God help them.

I might be a little bit crazy to think it, but I'm thinking I've found the girl I want to spend the rest of my life with.

And it just so happens that I don't care where we live.

If she wanted to move back to Houston, that might be a different story. I'd have to give that some serious thought. Serious, serious thought. But I don't see that happening. She seems to fit here.

She's making a home for herself. The threatening notes aren't helping, but otherwise, even with that going on, I think she likes it here.

I pull into a parking space downtown and park. Nothing is open yet, so I get out and walk around the little city park.

I'm looking forward to showing Audrey Whiskey Springs at Christmastime.

If Christmas was a town, it would be Whiskey Springs.

But right now, the trees have new growth on them. There are flowers popping up everywhere. Both the kind people plant in pots and the kind that spring up naturally along the edges of the path.

The river is swollen with snowmelt.

And endless cycle of winter, spring, and now summer. Fall is probably my favorite season. The leaves turn vibrant beautiful colors and flutter to the ground like silent raindrops.

I want to share all the seasons with Audrey.

Maybe I'm getting ahead of myself.

But I'm a Winslow and the Winslows go after what they want.

It's taken me a long time to find the woman that I want to go after.

And now that I've found her, I have to wait until she's ready. I don't mind.

Not even a little.

All in all, I think waiting is going to make us stronger and closer.

Maybe it's time I talk to her about how I'm feeling. I want to take the idea that I might be leaving out of her head.

Instead, I want her to be thinking about the possibility that I might be staying.

CHAPTER
SIXTY

Audrey

THE HOUSE ISN'T LIKE I was hoping it would be when my family started to come to visit.

I don't have the closets done or my office or all the little things that won't be obvious to anybody other than me. Like new door locks and window shades.

But when I see my sister's old car coming up the road, I realize none of that matters.

I meet her at the car and I can't hug her hard enough.

"You're crying," she says. "I knew we shouldn't have let you come up here by yourself."

"No," I say, wiping the tears away. "These are happy tears."

"Are you sure?"

"I'm positive."

"Okay then. Whoa." Audrey closes her car door and freezes. "There's a dog."

"That's Biscuit."

Biscuit is sitting several feet away. I'd told him to sit and stay. So he was doing just that. Sitting and staying.

Audrey glances from Biscuit to me, then keeps her gaze on the dog. "He's huge. Is he friendly? Does he bite?"

"I have to warn you. He licks. But he has such good manners. Biscuit. Come here."

Biscuits barks once, then runs over and, wriggling all over, standing next to me as though waiting for an introduction.

"This is Biscuit. Biscuit this is Lilah. My sister."

Lilah holds out a hand tentatively for Biscuit to sniff.

"I didn't know you were afraid of dogs," I say.

"I'm not. But that's more like a horse."

"Come on. Let's get you unloaded."

"Mom sent homemade cookies." Lilah reaches over and grabs a box from the passenger seat.

"When did Mom start baking?"

"I personally think they're homemade from HEB."

I shrug. "Close enough."

"I thought so, too."

"It looks like someone ate some of them."

"Someone might have. It was a long drive."

"I know. But I'm so glad you're here."

She pops the trunk and we drag out her luggage. She has paints and canvases on the back seat to get later.

"Did the dog come with the place?" she asks as Biscuit follows along beside me as we near the front porch.

"No," I say slowly. "I'm watching him for a neighbor." It's as close to the truth that I can get without telling her too much for right now.

She scrunches her face at me. "You hate neighbors."

"Hate is such a strong word. Anyway, it's different up here. Up here you have to have neighbors to survive."

"Sounds like you've moved to the wild west."

She has no idea. "It sort of is like that."

"I confess," she says as we reach the front door. "I'm a little concerned."

"Don't be. You're going to love the house. It's huge." I open the door to the inviting scent of wood smoke and cedar.

Biscuit trots in along with us.

"Biscuit acts like he lives here."

I close the door and lock it behind us. "He's a friendly dog."

"It's bigger than I expected," Lilah says. "And you've got a fireplace. Real wood?"

She leaves her suitcase in the middle of the floor and heads straight to the fireplace.

"I'm going to paint it," she says.

Biscuit flops down beside her.

"You can paint anything you want. Do you want coffee?"

"What kind?" she asks skeptically.

"The good kind." While Lilah sits in front of the fireplace, I go into the kitchen and make two lattes.

It's good to have my sister here.

I'm glad I came up here by myself. I don't regret that.

It was something I needed to do.

But I'm glad Lilah is here now.

Now I just have to figure out how to tell her that I'm not wanted here.

Not wanted here by someone unknown to me.

Someone who sees fit to leave me threatening notes about just how much I'm not wanted.

CHAPTER
SIXTY-ONE

Bradley

A FEW MINUTES in the General Store has me deciding on a teddy bear with a helium balloon.

"I'm glad to see somebody using this helium thing. The wife assured me that people would want balloons," John says as he airs up the balloon.

"They will. People just don't know about it yet. You should put it on your website."

John turns and stares at me, scratching his cheek. "Website."

"Yes. Put it on your website. Front page. Maybe run a discount."

John ties the balloon on the teddy bear. "Don't have a website."

"John," I say. "You need to get a website. Everyone has them now."

John makes a sound that I can't decipher and probably don't want to. "You sound like my wife."

"You should really listen to her, you know."

"Got this helium thing, didn't I?"

"Maybe you should put some balloons in the front window."

"You're right. Should have thought of that. I'm getting too old for all this modern stuff."

I don't have the heart to tell him that helium balloons are hardly modern.

"You want to buy a general store?" he asks.

"Me? No way. And you aren't selling." I swipe my credit card. "Just have one of the grandkids make you a website and you'll be fine."

He grumbles as he hands me the bear and balloon.

"Tell Claire I said hello," he says.

I hadn't told him the bear and balloon was for Claire. It bothers me a little bit that he knows this. But it's Whiskey Springs and not only doesn't everyone know everything about everyone, it would be poor form for me to visit anyone just coming home from the hospital without some kind of gift. It's not hard to figure out.

"I will," I say, heading out the door. "And listen to your wife." I add over my shoulder.

I have it on good authority that Claire actually came home last night. I didn't want to tell Audrey because I didn't want to drive out to Claire's last night and with her sister coming in this morning, I didn't want her fretting over it.

So I drive out of town, down toward Glenwood Springs where I happen to know that Claire lives.

She lives in a double-wide trailer on the outskirts of town. The trailer is hidden down a little road behind a grove of spruce trees.

The yard is clean, if not well-manicured. Not surprising since Claire lives alone.

I pull up beside her car and park. I really hope this trip is worth it and that Claire can provide answers.

Claire answers the door wearing a long, threadbare robe, her hair looking like it hasn't seen a brush in days.

"Bradley," she says. "Come in. I wasn't expecting company."

"It's okay," I say. "I won't stay long." I hand her the bear and balloon. "I got this from the General Store. It's from Audrey," I add quickly so she doesn't get the wrong idea.

"Oh. How thoughtful. I didn't know John sold balloons."

"We should help him get the word out."

"We should," she agrees. "And I'll tell everyone. Not that I see that many people. Have a seat."

I sit on an old threadbare sofa with an old cat curled up sleeping on the other end.

"That's Blackie," she says sitting on the equally threadbare recliner across from me. "He mostly sleeps a lot."

"It's okay. How are you feeling?"

"I'm so glad to be home. The Doc won't let me go back to work for another week though. I don't like putting Miss Audrey out like that."

"Audrey is okay. I promise she's not worried about you not being at work."

"Where are my manners, can I can you something to drink?"

"Thank you, but I can't stay."

"Are you sure? I can make coffee."

"I have some in the truck. I'm good."

"Okay. Well. I know you didn't drive all the way out here just to bring me this balloon."

"I need to know what happened that night. How did you end up unconscious on the side of the road?"

"It's the craziest thing. I'd just left Miss Audrey's, you know." I nod. "I'd slowed down for the narrows. And I saw these two kittens on the side of the road. I wasn't sure what they were at first. Thought they might be wild, but they looked like just regular kittens.

"I thought Blackie would love having some kittens around, so I pull over and get out. They take off. Of course. They run. But by then, I'm convinced they must be lost, so I follow them. I'm calling out to them, real sweet like. One of them stops and looks at me. That's when I know I'm doing the right thing. Poor little thing. All scared and hungry.

"Anyway. They take off again and I follow. It's dark and then..." She looks down and shakes her head. "I don't remember nothing after that. They said I slid down and hit my head. I don't know."

"I'm so sorry that happened to you."

"I'm just sorry I never got those kittens. For Blackie."

"I'll watch for them and if I see them, if they're tame enough, I'll bring them to you. How about that?"

"You are such a kind man. I told Audrey she needs to hold onto you. And I'll tell her again when I see her."

"Well. I appreciate that sentiment," I say. "And I especially appreciate you taking time to talk to me about what happened."

"It was no bother. None at all."

"So you didn't see anyone else? No other vehicles on the road?"

"Oh no. It was just me. Not very smart. I know."

"You have a kind heart. Do you need me to do anything before I head out?" I ask.

"I don't think so." Holding her bear and balloon, she follows me to the door.

"Keep your doors locked," I say.

"Will do."

She stands out on her little porch while I climb back

into my truck. I give her a little wave and she goes back inside.

Dead end. Audrey was right. Audrey had already figured out that Claire couldn't have left the second note, being in the hospital and all.

I didn't think Claire had left the notes, but I thought maybe she'd seen who did. But Claire hadn't seen any other vehicles. Even if she had, she probably wouldn't remember them. All she seemed to remember was chasing a couple of kittens she'd seen from the road.

I'll take a look around. See if I can find them. But they're mostly likely moved on to somewhere they can find food.

With that done, I head back toward town. I'll get some work done at the Bentley cabin while I wait to hear from Audrey.

CHAPTER
SIXTY-TWO

Audrey

Fortunately, Lilah loves the view from her bedroom so much that she doesn't question why I put her at the end of the hall.

"Oh wow," she says, standing at the window. "I can see everything from here. The river. The mountains with their snow-capped peaks. Is that a meadow? I love it. I can't wait to start painting."

"I thought you would like it. You can help me design your closet if you want to."

"That's your department," she says. "I can paint a mural on the wall, though, if you want me to."

"Let me think about that. Maybe."

By the time I finish showing Lilah around and setting her up in her bedroom, it's time for lunch.

"Do you want to drive into town? They have a great pizza place."

"Can we just eat something here? Maybe tonight. I'm just so sick of driving." She hides a yawn behind her hand.

"Sure. I can make some sandwiches. Then you can take a nap."

"You're the perfect sister. Don't tell Brianna I said that."

"Brianna who?"

Lilah laughs and takes a seat at the bar. The same seat where I had sat while Bradley made breakfast.

While I get out bread and ham and cheese and a tomato, I don't see Lilah open up my iPad.

"Why do you have this?" she asks.

"Why do I have what?" I ask, turning around to find her staring at the screen on my iPad.

My stomach drops. I know exactly what she's asking me about. She's asking me about the security cameras.

"Do you not feel safe here?"

"We just put those up yesterday," I say. "Let me get these sandwiches made and I'll explain."

After I throw together a couple of ham and cheese sandwiches and grab a bag of chips, Lilah and I head out to sit on the back deck to have lunch.

"I can't believe how cool it is out here," she says.

"I know. I doesn't take long to get used to it either." I set the tray of food down and Lilah sets down the iPad, then opens it up.

I reflexively glance around the tree line as I take a seat.

"I'm getting a bad feeling about this," she says. "We should have come with you."

"Lilah. You didn't need to come with me. I'm okay. It's just..." I open the bag of chips and hand them over.

"It's just you feel you need surveillance on the house. You must have put these cameras up for a reason.

"Yes. It's just that. Let me start from the beginning."

I tell her about the yellow daisies. About the first note that was left in a box. Then the second note that was left in an envelope.

"Can I see them?" she asks. "The notes?"

"The sheriff took them for evidence. But I took photos." I open up my phone and show her the photos of the notes.

"Okay. Somebody wants your inheritance."

"That's what's I'm thinking. So yesterday Bradley and Wyatt installed these cameras."

"Neighbors."

"Yes."

"And?"

"Last night I found another note tucked in my book."

Lilah looks me with a blank expression. "How long's it been since you looked in the book?"

"Not sure. I was thinking I read the night before, but I can't swear to it."

"I'm hoping you didn't. If you did, that means someone got past all this." She sweeps a hand over the camera images.

"I know." I bite my lip. "I have the note. It's upstairs. I'll show you later."

"Okay."

"But that's not all."

Lilah slides her plate aside. "There's more?"

"Nothing bad."

"Something good would be nice."

"The neighbor I told you about. Bradley."

"I remember."

"He's staying here until we get this figured out."

"Staying here?"

"Yes. In one of the other guest rooms." I don't look at her. I don't look at her because I'm remembering how Bradley had spent the night in my bed. A little different from staying in the guest room.

When Lilah doesn't say anything, I steal a glance at her.

She's grinning.

"What's funny?"

"Nothing," she says. "It's just I was picturing you up here all alone. I should have known something was up when you said a neighbor was helping you. You don't like neighbors."

"I like this one," I say in a low voice.

"When do I get to meet your knight in shining armor?"

"You want to meet him?"

Lilah looks at me sideways. "I'm thinking if he's living here, I'll should be meeting him."

"He's not living here."

"Okay." She shrugs. "Staying here."

"I guess tonight."

"Good. I don't like the thought of you being up here by yourself. I'm glad you've made a friend."

"Thank you," I say.

A blackbird lands on the deck and I toss it a chip.

"For what?" Lilah asks, watching the bird grab up the chip and take off with it.

"For not being judgmental."

"I am in no place to be judgmental."

"What have you done?"

"I told you. I got fired."

"And now you're here."

"Yes." She smooths back her hair, adjusting the scrunchy holding it back. "The lease on my apartment is up at the end of the month. I didn't renew it."

"Wait. Shouldn't you be home. Packing?"

"I haven't decided what I want to do just yet."

"Explain." I say it, sliding into my older sister mode. Something I haven't done since Thomas's accident.

She lifts an eyebrow, but she explains anyway.

"In some ways," she says, glancing around at the trees fluttering softly in the breeze. "I envy you."

"How could you possibly?"

"You get to start over. Somewhere new. You can be anybody you want to be."

"And yet I'm still me."

"Yes. Well. Maybe. It's sort of a choice, isn't it?"

I shrug. "Maybe."

"Imagine a world where you didn't tell anyone about your past."

"Are you wanting to reinvent yourself, Lilah?"

"I'm a twenty-three-year-old bartender. What do you think?" She tosses a potato chip toward a black bird. It picks it up and flies away with it.

"You're also an artist."

"Yeah. Well. It's not something I can exactly live off of." Her eyes look heavy and she yawns to prove it.

"Yet." I stack our empty plates. "Are you... wanting to move here?"

"I don't know." She raises her face to the warmth of the sun. "I guess I wanted to come out and see."

"And?"

She looks at me and smiles. "I probably shouldn't make a hasty decision."

"Probably not. I'll text Bradley. Let him know we're going out for pizza tonight. And you." I point at her. "You need a nap."

"I could just sleep right here."

"Up. You have a perfectly good bed to sleep on."

After herding my sister upstairs, I clean up the kitchen.

Not fifteen minutes later, Wyatt drives up with a load of firewood in the back of his truck. No trailer this time.

"Hey Wyatt. Is that for me?"

He steps out of the truck and pulls on his work gloves. "Bradley wanted me to top off your supply." He glances over at Lilah's car. "Your sister make it okay?"

"You could say that. She's upstairs taking a nap."

Was that a flash of disappointment that crossed his face? It happens so quickly I can't say for sure.

"Security cameras working out?"

"Yeah." I stuff my hands in my pockets. "I'm not so sure just how much good they're going to do."

"How so?" He leans against the truck door.

"Bradley didn't tell you?"

"Haven't talked to him today. What happened?" I see a fierceness in him now. I would not want to be on the other end of that expression.

"Another threat," I lower my voice, even though I have no reason. I already told Lilah. "Left it in the book I'm reading."

"Son of a bitch," he says. "Pardon my language. But there's no sense in that. If a man's got something to say, he should just say it."

"I agree. No need to apologize."

"I'm going to drive around. Unload this. Then get out of your hair."

"We're all going for pizza tonight. You want to come?"

"I can't. I've got a previous commitment."

"Okay. Next time then."

"Trust me. I'd much rather go for pizza." Back in his truck, he closes the door and tips his hat.

I smile as he drives around back.

Despite the obvious similarities between the two brothers, Wyatt is more wild-west. Maybe it's because Bradley graduated from Purdue. He's much more polished and could even pass for urban.

Not Wyatt. Wyatt is all small town.

Bradley is someone I could take to an art exhibit.

Wyatt is the guy to have on your side in a bar brawl.

They're as different as Lilah and I are.

SIXTY-THREE

Bradley

AFTER SPENDING the middle part of the day running new electrical wiring at the Bentley cabin, I stop by my place to shower and put on decent clothes.

Apparently, Audrey and I are taking Lilah into town for pizza tonight. Or maybe they're taking me.

Whichever way you want to spin it, the three of us are going.

I find it a little amusing that Audrey asked Wyatt to go. And even more amusing that my brother found an excuse not to go.

Wyatt talked big, but when it came right down to it, he chickened out.

My tough little brother is afraid to meet Audrey's sister.

Now that is funny as hell.

I get to Audrey's door and knock. I always knock. I'm a guest. One day... One day if things go the way I'm hoping, I'll live here, too, and I won't have to knock.

"Hi," Audrey says with a smile.

I'm so happy to see her smiling and not even realizing it, that I want to gather her in my arms and kiss her.

"Hi." Okay. Maybe I'm just looking for an excuse to kiss her. Any excuse will do.

"Come on in. My sister's still upstairs getting ready."

"It looks strange not having a fire going in the fireplace."

"I know. Speaking of. Your brother brought some more firewood. Are you trying to tell me something?"

"I just know how we like our fires."

She smiles and, biting her lip, catches me off-guard with a look that I can only describe as being a little bit flirty.

It's a cute look on her. One that has me spiraling down a road I honestly hadn't seen coming.

I'd been attracted to her from the moment I saw her. I knew I liked her.

I even knew I'd been thinking about maybe having a future with her.

But this... seeing her standing there, her hands in the back pockets of jeans that might be a little bit more filled out than when I first met her...

This has me thinking just how done I am. Audrey is the one. I have no more doubt about that.

"Sorry to keep you waiting." A younger, more light-spirited version of Audrey comes bounding down the stairs.

Whereas Audrey is dark and sultry, Lilah is light and airy.

She's right. They don't really look like sisters unless you know. They have the same build. Same long hair. Audrey is brunette. Lilah is blonde.

Lilah has a ready smile.

"It's okay," Audrey says. "He just got here. Bradley. This is my sister Lilah."

Lilah holds out a hand. "It's nice to meet you."

"You too." As I shake her hand, all I can think is that my brother missed out by not coming tonight.

Lilah is perfect for him.

I turn to Audrey and take her hand. It might look like a proprietary move, but it's my way of telling Audrey that she's the one for me.

We climb in my truck, Audrey in the middle, and I can't say I don't like the arrangement.

While I drive, I listen as Audrey tells Lilah about things we see. The steep ravine area that's not safe to drive when it's cloudy up here. How the currently swollen river that follows the road for a while flows downhill into Whiskey Springs.

She points out my cabin as we pass by.

"That's Bradley's cabin," she tells Lilah.

"A neighbor," Lilah says with a knowing nod. "but not too close to be a bother."

I suspect they have some kind of inside joke between sisters. Whatever it is, it's amusing to listen to.

"Is that your phone ringing?" Audrey asks me as we turn onto Main Street.

"Yeah. I'll check it later." I focus on finding a place to park outside the pizza parlor. It's crowded tonight.

"Friday night," Lilah says.

"You're right," I say. "I hadn't even realized it."

"I hadn't either," Audrey says. "The days just blur together up here."

My phone rings again as we walk toward the restaurant doors.

"It's the sheriff," I say. "I should answer it."

"Go ahead," Audrey says. "We'll get a booth."

Music spills out the door along with the sounds of people talking.

"Something wrong, Sheriff?" I ask, answering the phone, walking away from the noise of the pizza parlor, the phone pressed to my ear.

"We've had a break in the case," he says.

"A break? What kind of break?"

"I arrested Claire. For trespassing. And making threats. Stalking."

"Claire? Claire didn't do it."

"She did it. She confessed. And we got her prints on the notes."

CHAPTER
SIXTY-FOUR

Audrey

I KNOW something's wrong the minute Bradley walks into the crowded pizza parlor and sees us sitting in a booth across the room.

His smile is forced and he looks troubled.

"What's wrong?" I ask as he sits down next to me.

Bradley glances around. Makes sure no one is listening. "He made an arrest." He keeps his voice low. So low, even though he's sitting next to me, I have to lean close to hear him.

"Who?" I glance over at Lilah, wondering if she can hear us.

"Claire."

"Claire?" I look over at Lilah. "They arrested Claire." I tell her.

Lilah is shaking her head. She leans forward, her elbows on the blue and white checkered table. "Claire didn't do it."

"How do you know that?" Bradley asks her.

"It just doesn't add up." Lilah presses back against the booth and picks up a menu. "Sorry. I don't mean to overstep."

"How could Claire do it?" I ask Bradley.

"I don't know."

"I'll go talk to him tomorrow. But he said she confessed and her fingerprints were on the notes."

"That is so... unexpected."

"I know."

"Well. Maybe he knows something we don't."

"Maybe."

I'm beginning to think this was a bad idea. Coming to the pizza parlor. It's crowded and noisy.

But Lilah doesn't seem to be concerned about it. She watches everything. Takes in everything. I imagine she's seeing it with her artist's eyes.

"I hate we had to leave Biscuit home alone," I say.

"We'll get an alert on our phones if anyone approaches the house."

"I know. We just got one."

"Oh? I must have been on the phone. What was it?"

"Just a bird. Flying around the back patio."

"Oh. That reminds me. I was thinking we should put up motions lights around the house."

"You're adding to our list," I say, willing to let him add to a list that I've been making ridiculously long. Like heated bedroom floors and a gas fireplace in the bathroom.

"I don't think we're ever finish working on the house," he says, then tips back his bottle of beer for a swallow.

Something warms deep in my heart. Such simple words spoken nonchalantly. Words that mean so very much to me.

I glance over at Lilah, typing something on her phone now, then back to Bradley.

He looks over at me with an amused expression on his face. Lost in his light blue eyes, I search for something logical to say. Something that doesn't reveal just how much I'm feeling for him right now. "You don't think it was Claire either, do you?"

"I don't see how it could be."

"Take the note that was in my book. They can dust it for prints, too."

"I will. I'll do that."

I lean across the booth. "What do you think about this place?" I ask my sister.

"It's fun," she says. "I could get into it."

The server stops at our table. "What can I get for you all?"

We order a pizza to go with the beer that I probably won't drink.

"Lilah is thinking about moving up here. With me," I tell Bradley after the server walks away.

"Is that so?" He doesn't look at Lilah as he speaks. He looks at me. I see questions in his eyes.

Looking for answers to unspoken questions.

"It's a big house," I say softly, the words catching in my throat. I don't want him to move out.

Not because Lilah might be moving in and not because they may have caught the person leaving threatening notes.

Not for any reason.

"We still have lots of things we're working on," he says, finding my hand under the table and squeezing.

"Yes. We do." I don't know if he's talking about things to do around the house or things we're working on with us.

Maybe both.

But both the way he holds my hand under the table and his words give me hope that he's not thinking of moving back into his cabin.

I still haven't told him about the money I'm getting for staying there and I don't think he knows. He could know. It's a small town. All it would take is for one person to know and everyone would know.

I don't want to ask. I want to maintain the illusion for

a little while longer that everything will continue to be the way it is. Only better.

Having both Bradley and Lilah living with me in the big house sounds like the perfect life to me.

I'm getting ahead of myself. I'm still supposed to be grieving. Not planning my future. Certainly not a future with another man.

But, truly, who's to say that it wasn't part of a grand scheme?

Me getting married to Thomas. Thomas's accident. Me moving up here.

It's possible. Anything is possible.

SIXTY-FIVE

Bradley

WHILE AUDREY and Lilah are in the restroom, I check the security camera app.

The pizza parlor is noisy and crowded. Wouldn't normally bother me. But right now I want to have quiet time with Audrey.

It hadn't taken me long to get used to our quiet evenings at home. Cooking. Working on projects around the house. Sitting in front of her ridiculously big fires in the fireplace.

Just as Audrey had said, the motion was simply a bird flying close to the house. I zoom in to see it more closely.

Looks like a black bird hopping around on the back deck searching for crumbs. After a moment or two, it takes off.

Maybe by some odd quirk, Claire was actually the one who left the notes.

I don't get it. But then I'm not the sheriff. The sheriff is supposed to know what he's doing.

Either way, maybe Audrey and I can take a breather from being threatened.

We will see.

I'm willing to give the sheriff the benefit of a doubt.

I'm not, however, willing to leave Audrey alone. Not yet.

It is, however, hard for me to think about leaving her alone at all. For any reason. Threat or no threat.

Maybe I'd started out staying there with her with the intent of protecting her.

And I still have that protective instinct.

But it's grown. Now I just want to be with her whether she needs protecting or not.

The three of us pile in the truck and drive back to Audrey's house without incident. I find myself thinking about Wyatt again. Wishing he had come with us.

"I see why you don't like to drive up here," Lilah says, peering out the passenger window down the side of the mountain as we cross the precipice between Bradley's cabin and my house.

"And this is with a full moon. Right, Bradley?"

"That's right. I have a call out to a friend who's a civil

engineer about looking into putting rails up. But... I doubt the county will find it cost beneficial."

Lilah looks at Audrey. "You could probably pay for it."

"It'll probably cost upwards of millions to do it," I say.

"I don't think that's in my budget," Audrey says.

"That's not in anyone's budget." I pull around to the front door and kill the motor.

Suspect arrested or not, I can't help but look all around us. Even with the full moon, I can see no more than shadows in the trees. Someone could be lurking there.

I'd never really been on alert like this. Whoever had left those notes at Audrey's doorstep had taken away some of the peacefulness and safety I'd always felt in going about my day. I don't know if I'll ever get that back.

I hope I will and I notice Audrey looking around too, as she slides out of the truck on my side.

Hand in hand, neither one of us saying anything, we walk around and I open the passenger door for Lilah.

Somehow Claire just didn't strike me as the kind of person who would even think to leave threatening notes on anyone's doorstep, much less do it. She struck me as a simple woman more interested in taking care of her cat than...

"Claire has a cat," I say.

Both girls look blankly at me.

"I don't think she has any friends or family. Someone needs to take care of the cat."

"Call the sheriff," Audrey says. "We can keep her cat here. As long as we need to."

"Let's get you two inside. I'll call him."

Biscuit is so giddy with excitement, you'd think we'd been gone for days.

Lilah is a bit wary of him, but she'll warm up. Everybody warms up to Biscuit.

While Audrey builds one of her huge fires in the fireplace, I take Biscuit and step out back to call Sheriff Morgan.

"She's been ranting on about that cat all evening," the sheriff says.

"I can take it. Keep it here until she gets out."

"Alright. Come by the station in the morning. We'll drive out and pick it up."

"Will you tell her so she won't worry? It's just the humane thing to do."

"I'll tell her."

We disconnect the call and I stand there a moment, watching the breeze flutter through the trees. I get the feeling that alleviating Claire's mind about her cat is low on Sheriff Morgan's priority list. I'd bet money he won't even tell her.

That's a shame. Maybe Wyatt was onto something when he suggested I run for sheriff. Not necessarily me, but anyone other than Sheriff Morgan. Someone with compassion.

Maybe a lack of compassion comes with the territory.

It's hard for me to say. I'd been away at Purdue when Sheriff Morgan had become sheriff and he wasn't from here. So I couldn't say one way or the other about him.

It's such a beautiful night with the light of the full moon beaming down.

It gives me hope. Hope that Audrey and I can slide into a normal life now.

It's time I tell her what I'm thinking.

We don't have to be in any hurry. She can take as long as she needs for grieving the man she was married to before. But I want her to know where I stand.

That I'm interested in more just being here to protect her.

I want a life with her.

And it's past time I talked to her about it. Let her know how I'm feeling.

CHAPTER
SIXTY-SIX

Audrey

"That's a big fire," Lilah says.

"So I've been told."

Lilah sits curled up the sofa, a faux fur blanket over her shoulders, her eyes heavy.

I kneel in front of the fireplace, working on getting a fire going.

Lilah looks toward the back door where Bradley is pacing back and forth while he talks to the sheriff about Claire's cat.

The thought of that poor cat being left alone breaks my heart and I can only imagine how distraught Claire must be at the thought of having no one to take care of her cat while she's in jail.

I can't shake the feeling that Claire was wrongfully arrested. But she did have access. She had access to the porch before she left that night and she had access to my book. She also has a key to the house.

There's probably an explanation for the second note, though I can't begin to fathom what it could be since she was in the hospital at the time someone left it on my front porch.

No one saw her in the hospital.

Bradley went to see her and the staff denied that she was there. Claire doesn't seem like the type of person to turn away a visitor.

It makes my head hurt to try and figure it out.

"Bradley likes you," Lilah says.

"What makes you say that?" I glance up toward the back where he's pacing back and forth.

"I can just tell," Lilah says smugly. "And you like him."

"It's too soon for me to be thinking about anyone that way," I say.

"When it happens, it happens," Lilah says sleepily. "Never knew there were any rules. Maybe back in the 1800s, but even then..." She shrugs. "Nobody cares."

"Maybe," I say.

"Don't let worrying about what somebody might think keep you from following your heart."

I poke at the logs, watching the embers flutter up the

chimney. I hear what my sister is saying. And I know she's right.

"I don't think he feels that way," I say, but she doesn't hear me.

The back door opens and Biscuit rushes over to lie next to me on a rug I put down for him. I found the rug in one of the guest rooms and he loves it if the number of hours he spends on it is any indication.

"Okay," Bradley says coming from outside and slipping off his jacket. "Tomorrow we're going to have a visitor."

"Who?" I ask, trying not to cringe. Now that Lilah is here, I really just want to spend some time with my sister. And Bradley, of course, but that goes without saying.

"Blackie."

I look at Lilah. She shrugs and adjusts the fur blanket around her shoulders.

"Claire's cat," Bradley explains. "I'm going out tomorrow to pick him up.

"Good. Bring his food and litter box, too." I stand up and dust my hands off on my jeans.

"I will. Can I talk to you for a minute?"

"Sure."

He's still holding his jacket.

"Let me get my jacket."

"It's okay," Lilah say, stirring. "I'm going up to bed."

"You don't have to go. I just got the fire going."

"It's okay," Lilah says. "I'm asleep on my feet. I'll catch tomorrow's fire."

"Okay." I bite my lip, trying not to smile. She says it like having a fire in the fireplace is an event. I guess it sort of is.

Bradley hangs his coat in the coat closet and comes over to sit next to me on the sofa as Lilah makes her way upstairs.

"Something wrong?" I ask, grabbing Lilah's blanket and wrapping it around me.

"No," he says. "Everything is right."

"Oh. Okay." I slowly let out the breath I didn't know I'd been holding.

"I've been thinking and since I know it's not good to think and not share, I thought I should let you know what I've been thinking about."

"Okay. Sounds serious."

"Maybe." He straightens and leans forward toward the fireplace, his elbows on his knees.

The fire crackles and shifts, sending sparks flying up the chimney.

He holds out a hand and I put mine in his. He wraps his fingers around mine.

"I know it's too soon. Too soon for me to be thinking like I am. Too soon for you."

I forget to breathe.

My thoughts tangle up and I can't think.

"I don't want to just be here to protect you. I want to

do that, too, but I want more. I don't want to leave just because you don't need me here."

My eyes well with unshed tears. "I don't want you to go." I can barely get the words out past the lump in my throat.

He stills. Looks at me.

"Ever," I breathe, the word no more than a whisper.

"It's not too soon?" he asks.

"No." A tear spills from my eyes, down my cheek.

He leans forward. Kisses the one tear away, then another that follows.

With my heart swelling, a little smile tugging at my lips, I look into his light blue eyes.

"It's you, my love," he says, shifting to face me. "It's always been you. Even before I met you, it was you."

I put my hands on his shoulders and clasp my hands behind his neck.

He puts his hands on either side of my face and lowers his head until our breath mingles.

He presses his lips against mine and I melt into him. The world goes quiet.

Home. That's the word that resonates through my head as his lips move over mine.

His kiss is warm, certain, and filled with the kind of promise you don't have to put into words.

I sink into him, my heart daring to believe again.

It's not just a kiss. It's a beginning.

A promise whispered between mingled breath and heartbeats.

Home. That's the word that resonates through me as I melt into him.

Biscuit sighs and rolls over in his sleep, the soft sound grounding me.

For the first time since I lost everything, I don't feel alone.

And as his forehead rests against mine, I know this is the beginning of the rest of my life.

The End

AUTHOR OF JUST BREATHE
KATHRYN KALEIGH
Just
SURFACE
THE GRAVITY OF US SERIES

JUST SURFACE

PREVIEW

Chapter 1
Lilah Sinclair
Houston, Texas

I WOULD HAVE BEEN BETTER off taking a job as a showgirl.

Not that I knew any dance moves.

And learning choreographed dance moves would definitely have been more challenging than learning how to mix a Paper Plane cocktail and knowing the nuances of how that's different from the Last Word cocktail.

As a bartender, I'm not only required to know how to mix every possible drink, but also know a little bit of the history of each one. For example, the Last Word is a pre-

Prohibition cocktail that has suddenly become popular again.

People like it when their bartender can give them factual information. I only make it up about ten, maybe twenty percent of the time.

If I don't know how to mix a drink or some interesting fact about one, and I have time, my good friend Perplexity can help me out.

Fortunately, I have an excellent memory and I never have to look anything up more than once. So far. That, I am certain, is destined to change, simply because there are over ten thousand distinct mixed drinks.

Not to mention wines, beers, and spirits.

I work at two different bars. When I go in, I go all in. Besides, no point in not squeezing the most out of everything I'm learning about alcoholic drinks.

Tonight I'm at the Hobby Center. Only open when there is a Broadway event. Opening nights, like this, are my favorite. I love the elegance. The richness. The sophistication of it all.

With a tray of drinks in hand, I head off to deliver them to a group of well-dressed people who were standing in the far corner near the window when I left them.

I weave my way unobtrusively among the other patrons. Like moving furniture. No one notices the servers.

I find my group of three women and three men easily

enough. Separately, they all look stunning, but together, they make an unforgettable picture. The men are wearing black-tie tuxedos and the ladies are wearing sparkly evening gowns. All in their twenties, about my age.

And yet they obviously come from a world I can only dream of being part of.

There was a time when I somehow thought I would

I have no misperceptions that I landed this particular job at the Hobby Center in downtown Houston based on my bartending skills.

They hired me because I make people look twice.

No one notices the servers. Until they do.

I'm not particularly tall. An average five six. One hundred fifteen pounds. Long, healthy blonde hair that I'm supposed to wear loose around my shoulders when I'm out on the floor.

My work uniform is a black form-fitting cocktail dress. Very tasteful with a high neck and long sleeves. I've been told I wear it well.

I've even been told that I have a rich girl look, whatever that means. I assume it means my figure. Maybe a combination of my figure and my straight hair with just a hint of curl on the ends.

It helps that I have a ready smile. I sometimes wonder where I got that.

The figure and hair I come by honest. Both my sisters have a similar build with similar hair. My oldest sister has more of a serious sultry look and the middle sister wears a perpetual vexed expression that men, for some reason, find sexy.

I definitely came out ahead with my ready smile, in my humble opinion.

This particular group ordered champagne. Their loss and no challenge for me.

Holding my tray on one arm, I hand out glasses of champagne with my free hand.

Moving furniture.

The women take their flutes without bothering to acknowledge me. The men give me quick glances, artfully designed to not make their girlfriends or wives jealous.

I don't care. This is just a job for me.

"Hey," the slightly plump girl with blonde streaks says to me just as I lower my tray and start turning to leave.

I look at her with a pleasant, questioning smile.

She doesn't look the least bit familiar to me and she shouldn't. I've worked here for three months and I've only recognized a repeat customer a couple of times.

Honestly, they would recognize me before I would recognize them.

"Can I bring you something else?" I ask politely.

"You look familiar. Lily? Layla?"

"Lilah," I correct, feeling an unease creep along my spine. We don't wear name tags and there's no reason for this young woman to recognize me.

"Yes. That's it."

As though I don't know my own name. But I keep my

expression schooled in politeness. "Enjoy your evening," I say, starting to turn again.

"Didn't you date Trey?"

How could she possibly know this? "I think you have the wrong person." There's a time for honesty and there's a time for most definitely not admitting to something. This is the latter.

"No," she insists.

"Bernice," the man next to her says in a warning tone. "Let it go."

But Bernice does not appear inclined to let anything go.

"He told me about you."

"Enjoy your evening," I say again and this time I do turn around.

"He said you're a little too clingy for his taste."

Two steps away, I stop. My heart is beating like a jackhammer. But I take deep breaths and count to ten.

The man murmurs something to her.

She's had too much to drink. It happens. There's no need for me to take offense. I don't even know this woman and she has no reason to know me despite knowing my name and that I dated Trey for all of five minutes.

But Bernice follows me. I *feel* her following me. *Hear* her heels clicking on the marble floor behind me.

Then I sense her breath as she walks up behind me.

"Trey told me that you're a good lay, but you'll never

be more than that. Someone to just fuck when he feels like it. But he said he's not a garbage collector and you're just trash—"

I'll never really be able to explain what happened after that.

All I know is that I turn around, my fingers closing around the stem of a glass of red wine from the man standing nearest me and tossing it. I just toss it and the deep crimson liquid sails through the air. Right across Bernice's smug elegantly painted face.

Her gasp is sharp and wet, the wine dripping from her chin, running down her neck, and blooming in red blotches across her white silk blouse.

JUST SURFACE
PREVIEW

Chapter 2
Lilah

HALF AN HOUR LATER, I'm sitting in Natalie's office. Natalie is the boss. The big boss. Vice-President big boss. I normally would have to go through three other bosses to get to her kind of big boss. I don't think she was even here. I'm pretty sure they called her in. For this. For me.

My heart is still pounding faster than is natural, but I keep my gaze down.

I'm in a precarious situation and I know it.

Twenty minutes later, Natalie, in her perfect light blue

trim business suit walks in and leans against her wooden desk.

"Please tell me you have a good explanation for what happened," she says. She stares at me, her lips pressed tightly together.

"I—" I clear my throat and try again. "I do."

But Natalie doesn't seem to hear me. "I know it wasn't an accident. It's on camera. Do you want to see the footage?"

I shake my head. I really, really, really do not want to relive the moment.

Less than one hour. It only took one hour for my life to be flipped upside down.

"Do you know the definition of assault?"

I look up at her then, searching her eyes for some semblance of compassion. Anything.

I see nothing but coldness.

"I've never been in trouble," I whisper. From the look on Natalie's face, nothing about me or my history matters right now.

I should have called my sister while I waited for Natalie. Brianna would know what to do.

But I don't know her phone number and, besides, my phone is in my locker. I memorized hundreds of drinks and I didn't bother to memorize my own sister's cell phone number.

Brianna can bail me out of jail. I'm going to jail.

I straighten in my chair and raise my chin. My uncle is

an attorney. I can claim temporary insanity. Or permanent insanity. Whatever it takes.

Don't panic.

After making me sweat for what seems like an eternity, Natalie finally breaks the silence.

"Get your things out of your locker. Get out of here." She stands up straight. "Needless to say you're fired."

With disbelief, at being fired or not being hauled off to jail, I'm not sure, I stand up, feeling wobbly on my heels. I grasp the arm of the chair.

"You got lucky," Natalie says. "The girl's husband convinced her not to file charges."

"I don't even know her," I say as though that would work in my defense.

"All the more reason to not let her get to you. I suggest you find a different line of work."

I nod. I could not agree more.

I'm almost to the door when Natalie stops me.

"Lilah," she says.

"Yes?" I turn. I feel about two inches high and any kind word from Natalie. Any semblance of understanding. Would be a balm to my soul right now.

"Leave the dress."

I nod again and walk dazed back to the locker room.

I keep my eyes straight ahead. Fortunately I'm the only person back here. Everyone else is behind the bar or out on the floor working.

I never want to see any of these people again.

Grabbing my clothes out of my locker, I head to the dressing room. My hands tremble as I slide the dress off over my head and put on a t-shirt in its place.

I manage to hold my emotions at bay as I scramble into my jeans. Slide my feet into my sneakers.

The woman, Bernice, could have pressed charges. I could have gone to jail.

If Trey said those things about me. About me being trash, then all I'd done is prove him right.

By the time I make it to my car, tucked away in the far corner of the parking lot, my hands are trembling so hard I can hardly wrap my fingers around my key fob. I close the door, and the quiet slams into me harder than any insult ever could.

In the darkness, I lean my forehead against the steering wheel. The scent of wine still lingers on my fingers. And then the tears come. Hot. Unstoppable. Until I'm shaking too hard to breathe.

JUST SURFACE

PREVIEW

Chapter 3

Lilah

"Drink this," Brianna shoves a mug of hot tea into my hands.

"I don't need tea," I say. "I need a whiskey."

I didn't call Brianna on the way home from work. She called me.

We have a circle of friends and family app on our phone that alerted her that I had left work early. I hadn't even considered that when I'd finally stopped crying long enough to drive out of the parking lot.

As such, she'd known something was wrong before I even answered the phone.

"I got fired," I'd told her.

"What happened?"

"I'll call you tomorrow. I just want to go home and go to bed."

Being the older sister that she is, she was waiting for me when I got home. I pretended to be annoyed, but the truth of it was I was happy to see her.

The first thing I'd done when I'd gotten home was to wash off my makeup. The streaks of dried mascara down my cheeks took a special solvent to get off.

And now Brianna wanted details. *I got fired* was not nearly enough to satisfy her.

"Drinking isn't going to solve anything. We need to figure out your next move."

Déjà vu. Almost unnaturally so.

It's been less than a month since Brianna and I'd had a similar conversation with our oldest sister Audrey.

Admittedly, Audrey's situation was a whole lot more dire than mine. Even though... if I'd gone to jail... my situation could have been pretty dire.

"You can't compare this to Audrey's situation," Brianna says, sitting on the arm of the couch, breathing in the steam from her own mug of tea.

"You're being a freaky mind-reader."

"Audrey's husband *died*. You getting fired doesn't even compare. You'll get another job."

"I don't want another job."

"Right. You do know you have to work, right? Our family is not independently wealthy."

I look up at her with something that tells her I think she's wrong.

"No," she says. "You cannot count Audrey's inheritance."

"Stop reading my mind!"

"It's hard to not read it when you just put your thoughts out there like that."

With a huff, I sip my hot tea. Even though I won't tell her, she's right. The hot tea is soothing.

Sliding next to me onto the old comfortable couch I'd gotten from my grandparents, she picks up a stack of index cards on my coffee table. It'd taken plain index cards and turned them into flashcards. The name of a drink on one side. The recipe on the other. Riffles through them.

"You spent so much time learning all these mixed drinks."

I shrug. "Yeah. Well." It stings. I can at least admit to myself that it stings. I could have been doing what I really love instead of memorizing drink recipes.

She hasn't even seen the cards on my nightstand. Different kinds of wines and what they go with.

"You're good at it, too."

"It's good brain exercise," I say.

"That's for sure." She puts my cards back down, slips off her shoes, and curls her feet beneath her.

"At least you still have your other job. Maybe you can pick up more hours there. You said they tip better anyway."

I'm already shaking my head. "No. I don't want anything to do with bartending."

"But…"

To make sure she understands just how much I mean it, I set my mug down and pick up the index cards. Well over four hundred of them. I take them over to the garbage can in my kitchen and dump them in.

"There," I say, wiping my hands together. "It's done."

"Maybe you should sleep on it."

"I'm going to sleep on it," I say. "But I won't change my mind."

"You might be overreacting."

I slide back into my spot on the couch and pick up my mug. "I almost got arrested. I don't think I'm over-reacting."

Brianna just shrugs.

"It's not what I want to do anyway," I say.

"I know," Brianna says with genuine compassion. "But sometimes it's like that."

"You don't understand." I murmur.

"I've known you your entire life," Brianna says. "I think I have a general idea of what makes you tick."

"Then you know I'm not cut out to work in the service industry."

She looks at me sideways. "You say. And yet out of the three of us, you're the most cut out for it."

"Well then, we must all be pretty bad off."

Brianna leans back and closes her eyes. She has brunette hair like Audrey. Long enough to curl softly around her shoulders, but she keeps it pulled back, leaving just a couple of strands loose around her face.

In addition to her usual vexed countenance, she looks tired.

"You didn't have to come over here tonight. I'll be okay."

"You're lucky she didn't press charges."

"I know. Can she change her mind? Come back and press charges anyway?"

"Yes. She has a two-year statute of limitations."

"Oh. My. God." I cover my face with my hands. "I have to sit on pins and needles for two years hoping she doesn't decide to press charges?"

"Yes."

"What do I do?" I turn to my sister." You're a para-legal. You must know some way to resolve this."

"I do," she says. "You wait,"

I close my eyes. My life just became a living hell.

"But... you can get a good attorney. They have footage showing that she provoked you. She followed you across the room and provoked you."

"Slander," I say. "She slandered me."

"What did she say exactly?"

"I don't want to talk about it." I sit back and hide my embarrassment behind my tea mug. How had Bernice known exactly what to say to me that would provoke me into a haze of anger?

Brianna gets up, goes to my kitchen, and comes back with a little notebook and a pen.

"What's this for?"

"Write it down. Write down everything you remember. Word for word. I know they have the video, but you need to put it down in your words. Include what you were feeling."

"I really don't want to relive it."

"Do it anyway. You asked what you could do. This is a way for you to preserve your memory. Don't look at me like that. I know you have a good memory, but two years is a long time. Memories fade."

"Fine." I set my mug aside and start writing. Once I start, I can't stop. The words just flow out of me onto the page.

Finished, I close the notebook. "What do I do with it?"

"Just keep it."

Great. A tangible reminder of what happened tonight.

The neighbors, a friendly couple in their thirties, pull into the lot, their headlights sweeping across the pavement before clicking off. They climb out of their car, their voices low and intimate, as they walk past, carrying the kind of easy warmth that only comes from years of being together.

"So you're quitting your other job?" Brianna asks.

"Yes."

"And then what? How are you going to pay your rent? What are you going to live off of?"

"I'll figure something out. Just not tonight."

"Like what?" Brianna challenges.

"I can go back to school. Get a master's degree."

"Good idea. I think that's a good idea. How much money do you have saved up?"

"Saved?" I look at her like she's lost her mind. "I can hardly pay my rent and my student loan payments."

"Lilah." Brianna gives me with that long-suffering look of hers.

"I can sell my paintings."

"Maybe. Didn't you try that once before?"

"Yes. But I didn't keep at it like I should have."

"You're back to the idea of being a starving artist."

"Maybe. Although I'm hoping to be something more than starving."

"Okay." Brianna takes a deep breath. Lets it out slowly. "I hate the idea, but you can come live with me."

"No. I don't think so." I pick up my mug of what is now lukewarm tea. "I have a better idea."

"That's not a good idea and you know it."

"You don't even know what my idea is."

"I know perfectly well what your idea is. You're thinking about going to live with Audrey."

I hate it when she does that. "Just until I figure things out."

"That's what they all say. I really think you need to reconsider."

"Fine," I say. "I'm going to sleep on it." I stand up. Stretch. "Right now would be good."

I want tonight to just go away. I want to wake up in the morning and find out it was all no more than a bad dream.

But unfortunately, my older sister has other ideas.

JUST SURFACE
PREVIEW

Chapter 4
Lilah

"Lilah," Brianna says. "I know how much you love your art. Your painting and sketching." She looks around at the half dozen pieces of art I have displayed on my walls.

They're some of my favorites. But I can sell them if I have to. Anything to keep from going back to being a bartender.

The thought of walking back into a bar and working with the public makes me feel sick to my stomach.

"I know. It's not a real job." I sit back down and pull a throw around me.

Brianna is talking about my art now and it's like catnip to my soul. So I stay.

"Only a few people make a living at it. You can do it in your spare time. Like you've been doing."

What she really means is like I haven't been doing. Despite my good intentions, by the time I get home from working, I'm so exhausted, all I can do is fall into bed, then get up and do it all over again.

"We should call Audrey," Brianna says.

"No. We should not call Audrey." I don't want anyone else to know what happened tonight. I don't want anyone to know that I almost got myself arrested. I've never been so embarrassed in my entire life.

"You're going to have to tell her eventually," Brianna says.

"Why?"

"Don't ask stupid questions."

"Okay. I'll tell her I got fired. But not tonight."

"Okay," Brianna says. "Maybe tomorrow you'll wake up and decide that you can go back to the job you still have."

"The woman knew I'd dated Trey."

"Trey? That ass hat?"

"Yes." Brianna never liked Trey and obviously that has not changed.

"What did she say?"

I shake my head. I can't say it out loud. I'll never say it out loud. I'd rather die than tell anyone what Bernice said.

"It doesn't matter. But I'm never going to date again."

Brianna gives me one of her rare smiles. "You'll date again. You'll forget all about Trey. All about this night. And you'll date again."

"I don't think so. I've got two years for this to hang over my head. I can't be with someone and then suddenly get arrested. What would be the point? Just more embarrassment."

"Lilah. It's not the end of the world. Everything will look better in the morning. Whatever happens, you've got family support. You know that."

"I know." I blink back tears that threaten to spill over. I'd cried so much sitting in my car, I don't know where I could possibly have more, but here they are, welling in my eyes.

Maybe it's a sign to do what I've been thinking about.

"Will you help me pack?" I blurt.

"What?"

"Will you help me pack up this place?" I straighten, gesturing around my little one-bedroom apartment. "I've been thinking about moving and now seems like a good time to do it. My lease is out. I'm running month-to-month."

"Okay. I've got the day off tomorrow." She runs a hand over the arm of my couch. "If you're moving in with me, we'll need to sell your furniture."

"I was thinking I could put it in storage."

"A complete waste of money. By the time you're ready

to move out and get your own place again, you'll want new furniture."

I run a hand over the old threadbare linen-weave couch. "Okay. I'll sell it."

I'll sell my furniture, but I don't know that I'm moving in with Brianna.

Brianna lives in Houston and apparently one person too many recognizes me in Houston.

It's time for me to get away from here.

I've overstayed my welcome.

Keep Reading Just Surface...

Sign up for my NEWSLETTER to get all my romance releases, sales, Kickstarter announcements, and a **FREE** romance, SEALED WITH A KISS

CONTEMPORARY

The Gravity of Us Series

(Reading Order)

Just Breathe

Just Surface

Just Melt

Standalone Suspense

Out of Ashes

Alpine Falls (Maybe Yours) Series

(Reading Order)

Still Yours (Maybe)

Yours for Christmas (Maybe)

Forever Yours (Maybe)

(ALPINE FALLS)

Stranded in Alpine Falls

Belonging in Alpine Falls

The Spirit of Christmas in Alpine Falls

Christmas Wishes in Alpine Falls

Finding True North in Alpine Falls

A Ghost of Christmas Magic in Alpine Falls

Secrets and Second Chances

Honeymoon with a Stranger

Not Our Wedding

(SILVER PINES)

The Way Back to You

Back to Where We Began

When We Were Us

(ONCE UPON FOREVER)

My Forever Guy

Our Forever Love

Forever Vows

Finding Forever

Accidentally Forever

(TRUE NORTH)

Borrowed Until Monday

Still Mine

The Moon and the Stars at Christmas

Perfectly Mismatched

On the Way to Forever

A Merry Little Christmas

On the Way Home to Christmas

It was Always You

(UNBREAK MY HEART)

Begin Again

Love Again

Falling Again

(FOR THE LOVE OF THE FLIGHT)

Just Stay

Just Chance

Just Believe

Just Us

Just Once

Just Happened

Just Maybe

Just Pretend

Just Because

(MAGNETIC NORTH)

Second Chance Kisses

Second Chance Secrets

First Time Charm

Three Broken Rules

Second Chance Destiny

Unexpected Vows

(FALLING FOR CHRISTMAS)

The Heart of Christmas

The Magic of Christmas

In a One Horse Open Sleigh

A Secret Royal Christmas

An Old Fashioned Christmas

(CITY SKYLINE BILLIONAIRES)

Billionaire's Unexpected Landing

Billionaire's Accidental Girlfriend

Billionaire's Fallen Angel

Billionaire's Secret Crush

Billionaire's Barefoot Bride

(TRULY, MADLY, DEEPLY)

The Lady in the Red Dress

On the Edge of Chance

Sealed with a Kiss

Kiss Me at Midnight

The Heart Knows

(STOLEN ECHOES)

When Cupid's Arrow Strikes

Chasing Fireflies

A Chance Encounter

(EDGE OF THE HORIZON)

The Forever Equation

Pretend Boyfriend

All our Tomorrows

Kissing for Keeps

Out of the Blue

The Princess and the Playboy

(RED LIPSTICK KISSES)

Red Lipstick Kisses and Small Town Wishes

Stolen Dances and Big City Chances

Chance Connections and Upside Down Plans

A Christmas Kiss on the Twenty-Fifth

Believe in the Magic of Christmas

Vows of Inheritance Series

(Reading Order)

Vow to Protect

Vow to Redeem

ROMANTASY

(IN THE SPIRIT OF LOVE)

Spirits of the Heart

Out of Dreams and Ashes

Etched Upon the Heart

WESTERN ROMANCE

(LONE STAR HEARTS)

Wanted by a Texas Ranger

Saved by a Texas Ranger

(WHISKEY SPRINGS)

Finding Natalie

Promising Samantha

Falling for Allyson

Saving Savannah

Claiming Charlie

Rescuing Keira

Protecting Gabriella

Courting Isabella

TIME TRAVEL

(INTO THE MIST)

Written in the Wind

Scripted in the Stars

Destined in the Twilight

Promised in the Mist

Trapped in the Melody

(DRAGON'S BLOOD)

Dragon's Blood

Lavender Blue

Champagne Silver

Twilight Frost

Mountbatten Pink

(WHEN HEARTSTRINGS BECKON)

Rescued in Time

Meet me in 1879

(WHEN HEARTSTRINGS ECHO)

Messages Across Time

Falling Through to Forever

Once Upon a Winter's Spell

(BECKONED)

Before the Storm

Twist of Fate

When the Stars Align

Once Upon a Christmas

Once in a Blue Moon

A Wish Upon a Star

(BEGUILED)

When Lightning Strikes

Storm of Time

Midnight Storm

When the Moon Falls

Stormborn Angel

(SPELLED)

Time Tempest

The Heart Remembers

A Moment in Time

Moonlight Shadows

HISTORICAL

(TAPESTRY OF BLUE AND GRAY)

Shadows Beneath Magnolia Blooms

Secrets Among Southern Roses

(IT HAPPENED BY ACCIDENT)

Accidentally Alluring

Accidentally Married

(SOUTHERN BELLE CIVIL WAR)

Beyond Enemy Lines

Love Always

Hearts Under Siege

Hearts Under Fire

Away Down South in Dixie

The Reluctant Bride

Stay with Me

Jasmine Kisses

Magnolia Kisses

Gardenia Kisses

(THE QUINNS)

Wait for Me

Take Me Home

Keep Me Safe

FATED MATES

Riley's Mate

Aiden's Mate

Brayden's Mate

STANDALONE SUSPENSE

Lost and Found

All I Want for Christmas

Serenity

Courting Alley Cat

All of the books in each Series are standalone and can be read out of order. However, some books have characters from the previous stories in them.

9 781647 915278